GHOSTWRITER'S STUDY

a private investigator goes undercover

JULIE HIGHMORE

Published by The Book Folks

London, 2024

ISBN 978-1-80462-166-0

www.thebookfolks.com

THE GHOSTWRITER'S STUDY is the third standalone mystery in the EDIE FOX DETECTIVE AGENCY series by Julie Highmore. Look out for the first two books, THE MISSING AMERICAN and THE RUNAWAY HUSBAND. More details can be found at the back of this book.

For Sophie, James and Tom

PROLOGUE

She came around to the sound of raised voices. Actually, one raised voice, male, and a softly spoken female nurse. It was the old chap in the next bed, ranting in gibberish again. He might have been held in high regard at one time – a barrister, a popular greengrocer with the best local produce, an award-winning photographer. But now, poor man, he was tragically reduced to this. Of course, she could have said the same about herself. All those past accolades nobody remembers.

They were looking into her going home, she'd been told earlier. Installing a hospital bed in the drawing room and arranging for agency staff to pop in and 'sort her out' each day. She knew what that meant. Nappies. 'Tragically reduced,' she said and laughed. She'd always thought she'd go suddenly and dramatically. Her heel caught in a kerbside drain and a bus looming into view.

'Hello, Mum,' she heard, and her eyes opened to clinically bright light.

Then came another, 'Hello, Mum!'

'Sorry we couldn't get here earlier. The traffic was horrific.'

'Darlings!' she cried. Her children were here, how lovely. 'Do sit on the bed, dears. Either side of me. I know it's frowned upon but we're born rule breakers, aren't we? Oh yes, that reminds me, I would rather like to get something off my chest.'

Her cheeks were kissed and two chairs were pulled up. 'How wonderful of you to visit me,' she said. 'All the way from… Remind me, darlings, where…'

'You look pretty, Mum. Lilac suits you.'

'Thank you. It's funny how old ladies always take to violet! Now who was the poet who wrote about that? Or was it purple?'

'How was she last time you came?'

'The same. Not saying anything, sleeping a lot.'

'Remember how she loved to talk?'

'I know. It's odd, all this silence.'

'Of course I can talk!' She'd raised her voice like her ranting neighbour had. 'Just listen, will you? There's something I need to say…'

'Mum? What's the matter?'

'Is she trying to… Mum, are you trying to tell us something?'

She sighed with frustration and nodded. Then, lifting her right arm, she made a writing gesture in the air.

'Would you like pen and paper?'

'Yes please,' she said, adding a firm nod, just in case. Were her children going deaf?

'I don't have any paper.'

'Me neither.'

'I'll go to the nurse's station and ask for some. Might grab a coffee while I'm there. Would you like one?'

'No. Er, come to think of it, yes. Milk and sugar, please.'

'I'll be back soon, Mum!'

She nodded and said, 'Thank you,' then after a while heard a zip opening. A largish notebook appeared from a leather bag and she felt her fingers being curled around a metallic pen. She could just see her hand and the pen but not the notebook.

'Why don't you get the nurse to raise my bed a little?' she asked to no response, then felt the paper beneath the edge of her hand.

'OK, Mum. Ready?'

She nodded and began, as best she could, to form the unseen letters. First "TO" and then the name. Underneath, she concentrated hard, remembering the board game in which they'd had to draw clues for their team when blindfolded. She'd always been rather good at that task.

"I…" she continued, "AM… NOT… WHO… YOU… THI–" Suddenly, the paper was pulled from beneath her and the pen tugged from her grip.

'Nice try, Mother. Now let's concoct something less dramatic, shall we?'

She heard paper being ripped then watched as another note was quickly scribbled and torn from the pad.

'Here we are,' came an approaching voice. 'Paper, plus NHS pen and two coffees. Oh, you found some?'

'Sorry. I forgot I had my notebook with me today. Thanks for the coffee.'

'So, did Mum manage to write something?'

'She did. Here, look.'

'Aah, that's sweet. Think I might cry.'

The jagged-edged sheet of paper was turned for her to see. "Darlings" it said in spidery letters. "I love you both so very much. M xx".

'And we love you too,' they said in unison.

'Shall we take our coffees to the visitors' room? Let Mum get her beauty sleep.'

'Good idea.'

'See you after your nap, Mum!'

They said their goodbyes, while she stayed quiet. Why make an effort if they couldn't hear a thing? She lifted her arm in a weak wave and watched them stride off, then out of the corner of her eye spotted the other piece of paper and the NHS pen. They were on her moveable bedside table, the one she'd eaten meals off until she could no longer stomach them. Watery carrots came into her head and made her bilious.

If she could just write a note for one of the nurses to pass on… perhaps the friendly girl from… which country had she said? On stretching an arm as far as possible towards first the Biro, her fingertips brushed the side and she was able to roll it gently towards her and quickly secret it in her bed. She then reached for the paper that dangled over the edge, but as she grasped it, a shadow fell over her. The bedding was lifted, the pen retrieved, and the piece of paper was snatched and dropped into the leather bag.

'Naughty, Mother,' she was told, an unpleasantly damp kiss landing on her forehead. 'How devious you still are.'

ONE

After writing up a report on another wayward spouse, I sat back and swivelled in my chair, taking in the office I'd upgraded eighteen months previously, when partner Mike had finally put a bit of money into the business. We now had pale-oak floors, two cushioned client chairs and a comfy office chair for me, plus a few inoffensive prints, a tall leafy plant, and the orange armchair Emily used to breastfeed in when Flo was a baby. Yes, it was bland, but it no longer felt like a bedsit above a shop, parading as an office. I had no idea where the agency was headed, or how long it would last, but as long as it offered me respite from the family who'd moved back in with me, I'd carry on paying the rent.

Over breakfast, Maeve had talked again about finding herself and the kids a place to live. 'Somewhere close to Jack would be good,' she'd added. 'In south Oxford.'

'Oh?' I'd said, perking up.

Maeve had zipped up Alfie's lunch bag and handed it to him. 'It's just for practical reasons, Mum. We're not getting back together.'

'I know, I know.' If anything was going to stop Maeve reconciling with Jack, it would be pressure from me.

When the phone entry system screeched at me, I jumped and saw Emily on the screen. 'Edie,' she said, 'there's someone called Dylan here, asking if you might be free to see him?'

'Does he look like a serial killer?' I whispered. I was alone on the upstairs floor.

'Ha ha, not sure I've ever met one. Do you want me to come up and take notes?'

'Could you?'

'I'll check with the boss,' she said. Her brother, Oscar, managed the food store below. If I borrowed his sister mid-shift, I compensated him.

'Thanks, Em,' I said, then quickly cleared my desk.

A minute or so later, Emily – wild multicoloured hair, red polka-dot leggings, floral tunic and baseball boots – was followed into the room by a man wearing a three-piece grey suit and striped tie. It was a hot, early-June day and I hoped he wouldn't be overly warm in our small office. He was around five-nine or ten, with wavy blond-grey hair, sharp blue eyes behind black-framed glasses, a strong but not large nose, and a friendly smile. A rather nice whiff of cigar followed him in. We shook hands and exchanged first names, then he undid his middle jacket button, leaned his briefcase against my desk and took the seat I offered him. It was hard to put an age to him, but I guessed he was around sixty.

After introducing Emily as my assistant, I asked Dylan if he'd mind her taking notes.

He hesitated. 'Um…'

'What you tell us will be strictly confidential,' I assured him.

I took my pen and notepad over to Emily in her armchair. She'd normally write straight onto her phone, so didn't look too pleased. 'And Emily's notes will only be typed up with your permission. If you decide not to employ us, you can take the notes with you.'

'Sounds fair enough,' he said. 'I plan to give you only a bare outline today.' His voice was deep, but at the same time quiet.

'OK,' I said. 'How can we help?'

'I'm here about my sister. Suzie.'

'Sorry,' said Emily, hand in the air. 'Is that with *S* or *Z*?'

'With a Z.'

'Cool,' she said, writing it down. Emily had that unsettling way of holding a pen young people now used, involving almost an entire fist. It was putting me on edge, but since she rarely wrote anything I just needed to chill.

'Suzie's my older sister,' continued Dylan. 'There are only the two of us, and our parents have both passed away. I live in London and Norfolk, but she's here in Oxford and has been for decades.'

'Uh-huh,' I said to his mellifluous tones.

I wanted to be taking notes as well, just for something to do. But I would have had to rummage in a drawer for another pad, and thereby look unprofessional. My last ex, Billy, had more than once hinted that I might have an attention-deficit problem. But since he'd been a unitasker of the highest order – 'How can I listen to you when I'm buttering toast!' etc. – I hadn't taken it seriously.

Dylan took a deep breath. 'OK, so, over the past few years my sister has experienced various health issues. I won't list everything but she had a fall two or three years back and broke her right hip. Then, having struggled to regain mobility after a hip replacement, X-rays showed arthritis in her other hip, and the following year she had to have another replacement. She'd learned her lesson though and this time did all the exercises. She's pretty mobile now.'

'Oh good,' I said.

'There are one or two other issues that come with aging, but she's on medication and generally doing well, physically.' Dylan leaned forward. 'What I'm becoming a little concerned about, though, is her memory.'

'Ah.'

'Short-term. Her long-term memory is phenomenal.' He chuckled and shook his head. 'And believe me, Suzie has some pretty awesome distant memories.'

'Oh, really?' I said, beginning to wonder if he'd mistaken us for care providers. I hoped not because that would have been embarrassing. 'Does your sister have any children?'

'No, sadly. She and her ex had wanted them, but it never happened. Suzie's been a wonderful aunt to my daughter, though. So, anyway, since I'm mainly in London, and occasionally Norfolk, and my work is relentless, my daughter and I organised live-in help for Suzie. This was back when she had mobility problems and found the stairs particularly difficult. She lives in a large house that she was given as part of a settlement decades ago. Suzie was with someone in the music industry, who was very successful and had several homes, here and abroad. The Oxford house was bought for nostalgic reasons because Suzie had gone to boarding school in the city from age eleven. Although our roots are in Norfolk, she always felt more at home here.'

It was no good, Dylan had the voice and gentle delivery of a hypnotherapist. I needed to write or doodle, in order to keep myself alert. While I asked if he'd like a drink and listed what we had, I casually pulled a notepad from my bottom desk drawer and found a pen from the top one.

Dylan said he was fine, thank you, and continued. 'Suzie's house has some very nice spare rooms, so my daughter and I advertised for live-in carers and got six applicants. Together with Suzie, we interviewed a shortlist of three women, and the one man who'd responded to the ad. He came with an impressive CV and glowing references, and completely charmed us all. Suzie took to him instantly. We'd decided on two employees, a cook and a carer, and he got the carer position.'

'And the other person?'

'Well, Suzie has never been a keen cook. Not since a home economics teacher said if the Spanish had fired Suzie's jam tarts at Trafalgar, we may well have lost.'

'A bit harsh.'

'Indeed. Anyway, Suzie was most impressed with an applicant in her mid-thirties who'd been a chef on various yachts for years and just wanted something more stable. If you'll excuse the pun.'

I smiled and asked if they'd stayed on, once Suzie had recovered.

'Yes, luckily for me. She'd adored them both from the start, then became more and more attached. I must say this arrangement has brought me welcome peace of mind over the past few years. Until now.'

'Why until now?'

Dylan leaned in again. 'OK, so two things have happened in recent months, which have brought me here. One is that items appear to have gone missing.'

'Oh!' I said, jolted out of the idyllic set-up Dylan had painted. 'Such as?'

'Antique ornaments, jewellery, some clothes and a garden statue, apparently. I don't know the full extent because the place is pretty much packed to the gills. Plus, I don't have a great visual memory for things, places, and so on.'

'My brother's like that,' Emily said through a yawn. 'Oh dear, 'scuse me. Yeah, so Oscar has to have all his tins and packets of food with the name facing out, or he can't find whatever he's looking for and has a meltdown.'

'Me too!' said Dylan. 'Well, not the meltdown bit. Luckily, my daughter has made a list of items she's noticed are missing.'

‘That’s good,’ I said. ‘And the second thing?’

Dylan sat himself more upright. ‘For a long time Suzie’s been talking about writing a memoir, or a bit of a tell-all as she calls it. English was always her best subject but now… let’s just say she’d struggle to write it herself. Anyway, I did say, a while back, that I’d try to find her a ghostwriter, but to be honest I did nothing about it. I think I was afraid of libel actions, since she’d mixed with some well-known people for a while.’

‘I see.’

‘Suzie’s brought up the memoir idea every time I’ve spoken to her recently. I think she’s becoming aware of her memory issues and wants to put things down on paper before it’s too late. She can get quite emotional about it, and has even threatened to pay her male carer to help her write it. Obviously, we don’t want her pouring out scandalous allegations to just anyone, or even to a professional ghostwriter. So… well, my daughter and I came up with a solution.’

‘Which is?’

‘We pretend. And by pretending, we might kill two birds with one stone.’

I expected an ‘Aww, poor birds’ from animal-loving Emily, but when I looked over she was asleep, pen poised on the A4 pad about to fall off her lap.

Dylan followed my gaze and whispered, ‘Is she OK?’

‘Emily has a toddler,’ I whispered back. I wondered if she’d benefit from a Dylan relaxation session every day.

I pointed at the door and made a drinking-coffee gesture. He nodded, then together we tiptoed out of the office and went to the café next door.

By the time we sat down with our drinks, I’d worked it out. ‘So, you’d like one of us to pose as a ghostwriter, whilst keeping a close investigator’s eye on the staff and any visitors?’

‘That’s exactly what I’d like.’

‘I do have a few questions.’

'Go on.'

'Does Suzie have a partner?'

'Romantic? No. There were two short-lived relationships following the musician, and one or two flings, but since she was patently still in love with her ex, none of them worked out.'

'Does she still see him? Are they in touch?'

Dylan shrugged. 'It's possible she still sees or hears from him, but I was never a massive fan, so I'm pretty sure she wouldn't tell me.'

'Can I ask why you're not a fan?'

'He didn't marry her, and I thought he should have. Oh, there was some ceremony, on a beach in Goa. I'm convinced Suzie thought she'd got married. She changed her name to his, but the marriage wasn't legally binding in the UK. They were a pair of feckless hippies, basically, and he wasn't particularly generous when they split up. Suzie would have done a lot better as an ex-wife.'

'I see. This is pure nosiness, but is he still in the public eye?'

Dylan paused before answering. 'Would the main stage at Glastonbury count?'

'Blimey!'

'I don't want to name names, right now,' he said. 'However, should you take on this unusual assignment you'll be filled in on absolutely everything, and not necessarily by me. My sister is quite a talker.'

'The perfect subject, then. Also, what would you want done with all the information Suzie gives me, or whichever one of us takes on the role?'

'Actually, I'm hoping it will be you. It's probably best if a biographer stays awake?'

'True.'

'What I'd like,' he said, 'would be for you to forward all recordings and notes to me after each session. Or, better still, I'll organise a courier to collect them from you. Then my daughter and I can decide what to do with them. We thought of having one book printed, which we could give her, but she's currently too switched on for that to work. Sorry if that sounds callous, but we have her best interests at heart. Ultimately, I don't think it will get anywhere near that point. My sister rarely sees things through, so chances are her enthusiasm will wane.'

'You're more concerned about the missing items?'

'Yes. And whether the problem is even bigger, like financial shenanigans. Suzie's a bit drifty, but she's always invested wisely and kept on top of her money. I can't be sure that's still the case. I've attempted to talk to her about it, but she tells me everything's tickety-boo. I've searched through drawers and places for printed bank statements, but have only come up with old ones, dating back to before the carers moved in. She doesn't seem to have a banking app on her phone, and there are no signs of online banking on her laptop or PC. I can't help wondering if someone else is in control, despite the carers claiming no knowledge of her financial situation. Obviously, I'd need power of attorney to check her accounts via the bank, and that can only be initiated by Suzie herself.'

'I can see why you're concerned,' I told Dylan. 'And I'm sure we'd be able to help.'

He smiled at me, lightening up at last. 'It's a bit of a long shot that may or may not produce results. If at any point you were to feel uncomfortable, or think your cover's blown, you could always bow out and I'll attempt the power of attorney route.'

'Could I talk it over with my colleagues later today?'

'Of course. How many of you are there?'

'Three.'

He gave a nod of approval. 'Nice and small. You have good testimonials online, which I trust are real?'

I had no idea. Mike maintained the website. 'They are.'

'Excellent.' Dylan picked up his briefcase. 'I'm going to have to shoot off, I'm afraid. Promised Suzie I'd arrive before lunch. I'm staying there tonight.'

When he stood up, I did too and we walked out of the café and lingered awkwardly on the pavement. I was waiting for him to at least give me his phone number.

'You and the others mull it over,' he said, 'and I'll pop into your office tomorrow before I head back to London. Perhaps you'll have more questions that I'll try and answer.'

'OK. When will that be, roughly?'

'Is around the same time OK?'

'Um... one moment.' I got my phone out and pretended to check. 'Ye-es, that should be fine.'

'OK, well, great meeting you, Edie.'

'Nice meeting you too.'

He gave a small wave and strode off, but then turned around. 'So *do* I look like one?' he called out.

'Sorry?'

'Maybe lower the volume a tad on the intercom?'

TWO

Emily came up to the office after her shift and had apologised ten times before Mike arrived a couple of minutes later.

'Enough!' I told her.

'Enough what?' asked Mike, and Emily told him.

'It really wasn't a problem,' I said. Again.

'Jesus, Em,' said Mike. 'I'm amazed you're awake as much as you are. Seth and I had his six-year-old nephew one Sunday and I had to cancel all my Monday lessons.'

Emily giggled. 'Whatever you do, don't you and Seth go thinking about having a baby.'

'Yeah well, zero chance of that at the moment. Anyway, can we talk about the new job, as I'm teaching at five.'

Mike had been much busier in recent months, having set up a tutoring agency. He'd continued to teach one-to-one, but was now raking in his cut from the other tutors who'd paid to register with him.

I filled them in on Dylan and his proposal. 'What do you make of it?' I asked. 'Em?'

'Not sure,' she said. 'I mean how ethical it is to go and con some poor woman with no real hips, who's, like, putting books in the fridge?'

'Mm,' I said. That had crossed my mind. 'Mike?'

'I think fuck the ethics and let's stretch this job out for a year, then keep the notes and recordings you'll duplicate for us, and sell the biography to a publisher using a nom de plume.'

'Cool!' said Emily, perking up at the mention of money. She and her police-officer husband, Ben, were hoping to upsize from a flat to a house. 'We could, like, make one from all our names? Come to think of it, middle names would be safer. What's yours, Mike?'

'Thomas. Officially, I'm Michiel…' He spelled it out. 'Thomas Wilders. Pronounced Vilders.'

'Ooh, sounds posh.' Emily looked my way. 'And you're Edie Marie?'

'I think we might be getting ahead of ourselves, but yes.' I'd never liked either of my names as a child, and had longed to be a Sarah, or Anna, or Beth, or Hannah, or Georgina. But when I got to Oxford everyone had those names and I finally felt happy with Edie.

'My middle name's Josephine,' said Emily. 'So, how about… Marie Josephine Thomas? Or M J Thomas?'

'Not bad,' said Mike, 'but back in the real world, do you think there'll be any part Emily and I can play in this? I could pose as an electrician, or plumber. General handyman.'

'I reckon we should just go with the flow,' said Emily. 'That's my favourite Zen tarot card.'

Mike checked the time and swore. 'There's a flow I really need to go with. But it's a yes from me, Edie.'

'OK. Good.'

'Keep me posted,' he said with a wave.

Emily told me she had to go too, as her mum and dad were with Flo in the flat. I almost made a joke about going to the Flo.

'They're teaching her to read and write,' she added, 'and it wears her out, poor thing.'

'But she can't even…'

'Talk? I know. They're just like trying to make up for messing up my education, and therefore my entire life. Well, until I met you, then through you, Ben. Anyway, they keep telling me Flo's a total genius, but I can't say we're seeing it.'

'I expect your parents are well-meaning.'

Emily laughed. 'If a bit shady.' She got out her phone and showed me a video of two-year-old Flo writing "I love you Nanny" inside a card. 'Look, you can just see Mum's hand guiding her little wrist.'

'Oh yes…'

'Bless her.' Emily hooked a bag over her head, pulling her long colourful hair out from under the strap. 'I'll be in the shop tomorrow, so let me know how it goes?'

'I will. Oh, while I remember, could you ask Oscar if he knows how to turn down the volume on the entry-phone?'

Emily sighed, leaned over me and did something with the contraption on my desk. 'Honestly, Edie. I thought you boomers burned your bras and wanted a world without men?'

'I'm actually…' I said, but she was already laughing her way down the stairs, and besides, I couldn't quite remember what I was. Gen X?

* * *

I left the office around six, picked up some things from the deli-cum-general store downstairs, and walked along the buzzing Cowley Road towards my house.

East Oxford is a half-mile-long triangle of Victorian and Edwardian properties, containing a mix of students, young professionals with children – and generous parents – and retired university lecturers who bought their houses for a song in the eighties and haven't moved on decoratively. The pointy bit of the triangle is just yards from Magdalen College and Oxford High Street, which explains the ludicrous house prices.

On the way, I thought about Dylan's unusual proposal and suddenly wanted to talk to my friend Astrid about it. I also wanted to find out how the newly divorced Astrid was coping in the far-less-grand house she'd had to settle for, in order to keep her only child, Jakob, at his local school – and also because she was officially broke. I messaged her asking if she wanted to meet for a drink at the Oxford Scholar later. "Half eight?" I suggested.

Last time I'd seen Astrid she'd cried; something I'd thought her incapable of. I'd asked if she was missing Jonathan – her lovely, tolerant and handsome ex, who still completely adored her – and she'd looked at me bewildered. 'You know I have to stand in the bath to take a shower?' she'd said, nose in a tissue. 'It's positively barbaric.'

My phone pinged. "Yes" was her reply. I assumed Jakob was with his dad.

Turning the corner into my street, I found myself growing tense. I'd recently noticed that things were often calmer and more fun when Maeve wasn't home, and I had Alfie, now eight, and three-year-old Betty to myself. The day before being an example. After a fraught and chaotic activity-filled Saturday, Maeve – whose weekend it was to have the children – had decided to spend Sunday afternoon working in the library. While the cat was away, the three of us had watched *The Bad Guys* movie and eaten pizzas. 'Our secret,' I'd told them.

* * *

'Oh, Edie,' said Astrid. 'What have I told you about wearing duck-egg blue?'

'Hi, Astrid. Lovely to see you too.'

We air-kissed and I pulled out a chair. The Scholar was surprisingly busy for a Monday and music competed with the roar of voices. I was tempted to suggest we go somewhere quieter, but since passing fifty I'd been careful not to say things like that to her. Astrid was halfway between Maeve's age and mine, and Jakob was the same age as Alfie. At first, Maeve had been Astrid's friend, when their boys were babies and toddlers. But then I'd found myself stepping into that role after Maeve finally fled the friendship, wishing me luck.

'Not too loud for you?' she asked with no sign of a smirk, or in fact any expression at all.

'No,' I yelled back, my voice already raspy. I leaned in towards her. 'Have you had Botox again?'

'I have.'

'But I thought you were hard up?'

She knocked back the rest of her wine. 'Along with Harrods Lapsang, and a decent hairdresser, oh and the odd bit of weed, I consider it one of life's essentials.'

'Fair enough,' I said. 'And you do look great.' With her straight naturally blonde hair and her skinniness, she always did.

'Good,' she said, 'because I've invited a friend, well someone I met at the gym today. Oh, and he's bringing a friend for you.'

My heart and mood plummeted. All I'd wanted was a couple of drinks and a natter with her. On top of that, I was wearing an unflattering colour. And how old would these dates be? Had Astrid noticed I was now over fifty and finally having to touch up the grey in my naturally dirty-blond hair? Or that I was in good shape for my age, but perhaps not for someone her age? Or that I did in fact have a partner? Sort of.

Astrid pointed to her empty glass. 'If you're going to the bar, I'll have their most expensive red.'

I stood facing the sea of bodies and contemplated walking around it, then through the passage to the loos and slipping out the side door to the street. I could go home and watch house flippers on YouTube, or that woman who's brutal to failed hoteliers.

'A large one!' called out Astrid.

* * *

After an hour-long attempt to show interest in the benefits of getting up at five every morning, I was desperate to leave. The first ten minutes or so with my sandy-haired, way-too-young blind date, had actually been fascinating. Cold-water swimming at 6 a.m., how admirable, if incomprehensible. Later, fatigued by the health stats, I'd tried and failed to bring in other subjects – my family, his family – but the boy was relentless.

I finally gathered my things and got up. 'So sorry but I have to go and babysit. Nice meeting you, er…' Alistair? Anthony? I gave the three of them a small wave and my date did a thumbs up. Astrid looked disappointed in me, or maybe she didn't. So hard to tell.

As I walked home, I braced myself. It had been an adjustment for everyone after Maeve had split up with Jack and left Brighton ten months previously, letting the large house her father had indirectly bought for her. A new school for Alfie, a new course for Maeve, and rather too much company for me. But, I reminded myself, the important thing was that Maeve seemed happy again, following a post-natal dip.

For a while, Jack – wanting to still be in the kids' lives – had slept in the garden room. I'd personally rather liked that arrangement. He and I would sympathise with each other when Maeve was being tricky, and he'd been on hand to hold the fort, take Alfie to school, or cook a delicious meal. With Maeve studying again, he'd been a godsend. It was never going to be a long-term thing, though, and he was currently renting a flat off Abingdon Road. Not far away, but not the same.

Even before entering the house, I heard Betty wailing. Inside, Maeve was carrying her daughter around the open-plan room, rubbing her back and saying, 'It's OK, Bets, *The Bad Guys* aren't real. It's just a film, honey. Just made-up drawings of funny animals. There, there. I'm sure Gran's *really* sorry she let you watch it.' Maeve glared over her shoulder at me. 'Especially as the film came with a warning of scenes that would scare or disturb some children under five.'

As Betty sobbed her way back to bed, I made a beeline for the fridge and retrieved the bottle of wine I'd hidden behind the now-permanent mountain of vegetables. I poured myself a glass and sat at the island with my laptop. "Homes to rent Oxford" I googled, unsure if I was looking for Maeve or for me.

THREE

The following Monday, feeling both nervous and excited, I walked onto the gravel drive of a north Oxford villa, which is basically what they call a house up there. In the taxi, on the way, I'd thought through what Dylan had shared with me. Just the very minimum, actually. Said he didn't want me slipping up early on and someone guessing he'd hired me, then them finding out who I really was. I wasn't even given Suzie's address until I was in the taxi Dylan had booked for me.

When we'd met again and I'd agreed to take on the job, he'd asked what name I'd like to use.

'How about Marie Josephine Thomas?' I'd asked.

'Good, yes,' he'd said. 'I'll organise some ID.'

Then, at some point, my existence in Oxford had magically appeared on Suzie's radar. I wasn't told how. Suzie had then called 'my assistant' and arranged the meeting I was on my way to. It had been a convoluted smokescreen that managed to hide both her brother and the real me.

On the villa's front drive, I passed a white Audi and two bicycles, all parked in the shade of a tall hedge. I stopped and looked up. The detached house was bigger than some primary schools I'd taught in. It was double-fronted, as in a child's drawing, and was constructed from a mellow-yellow brick. A pitched-roof side extension, made of slightly newer-looking brick, housed a garage with a deep-red door. The main house had three floors, one of which, judging from the small gabled windows, was in the attic. The square shape of the ground-floor bays meant it probably dated back to the early nineteen hundreds.

In amongst the blanket of ivy cover, I spotted a blonde-haired woman waving from the first floor. She lifted the bottom half of a sash window and called out, 'Are you Marie?'

I told her I was.

'I'm Suzie. The front door's on the latch, sweetie. Do come up to the drawing room.'

When I let myself into the house through the heavy oak and stained-glass door, I was met with a large, square, beautifully tiled entrance hall containing a pretty piece of furniture that probably had a French name. It was covered in keys and scarves, hats, flyers and letters, two bike helmets, and much more. Beyond it was a gorgeous wooden art deco carver chair with slim arms and a tall beautifully detailed back. Somewhere to sit while putting on or tugging off shoes and boots, I imagined. Beyond that was an ornate black-and-gold umbrella stand, holding walking sticks.

Above all of these things, on the wall, was a mixture of paintings, posters and photographs, including a photo of a younger Dylan. Perhaps in his thirties. He wore a dinner jacket and held up a champagne glass, as though making a toast. Dylan had brought family photos to my office, as proof that he really was Suzie's brother, but it was good to see further evidence.

On either side of the entrance hall were closed doors to the two front rooms, and in the distance was a wide staircase curving upwards. As I walked towards it, someone appeared at the top and came bounding down.

'Hi, Marie,' said a baby-faced guy of medium height. He had twinkly blue eyes and fair wavy hair that was fuller on top than at the sides. Because people now looked young for so long, I put him somewhere between twenty-two and forty-two. 'I'm Joey. Here, let me carry your bag.'

'Thanks,' I said, handing it over.

It really wasn't heavy. Today I'd packed only a notebook and two pens, a cardie and a purse. Since this was going to be an informal chat, I'd felt no need to bring the retro cassette recorder Dylan had provided me with, nor the new laptop he'd preloaded with email, Word and several subscriptions set up in the name of Marie Josephine Thomas. I did have the fake driving licence in my purse, though, along with a fake bank card. These were in case someone rifled through my things. How Dylan had acquired those I didn't ask. I had two phones on me too, my real one being hidden in my false-bottomed bag, covered in bubble wrap. It all made me feel rather like a spy, which of course I was.

I felt the rear pocket of my black jeans to make sure my real bank card was still there, then looked back at the front door. 'Should we lock it?' I asked.

'Nah, no need. We're always in and out, and anyway if someone wandered in, they'd have Dolores to contend with. She does all the cooking and has what you might call a chef's temperament. Oh, and lots of sharp knives.'

I laughed. 'OK. Good to know.'

'Here,' he said, pulling a set of keys from his pocket. 'I'll leave these out for you to take.' He put them on the French thing and chuckled. 'If Suzie likes you, that is.'

And there was I thinking I already had the job. 'Fingers crossed!' I said, still smiling.

Joey pointed towards the door on the left as you came in. 'That's Dolores's room. And opposite is mine. We kind of guard the palace, while our queen mostly reigns from on high.'

'Shall I take my trainers off?' I asked, spotting a shoe rack beneath a row of coats and jackets.

Joey looked down. 'No, you're all right for today. But you could always bring indoor shoes in future? Apparently, it costs a fortune to clean Suzie's precious rugs.'

As I followed Joey towards the stairs, I saw to my left that the rear section of the hall wall had been knocked down to create an open social and kitchen area of quite some size. It wasn't super neat and state of the art, like many opened-up kitchens – how, in fact, mine had looked before Maeve moved back. Here there was a mix of dark-blue and bright-green kitchen cupboards, and, yes, an expensive-to-clean oriental rug. There were sheepskin-strewn wicker chairs, lots of plants, a massive Welsh dresser, and a long chunky wooden table with assorted chairs around it. The aroma of a cooked breakfast hung in the air, and from the bottom of the stairs, I caught sight of a fair-haired person bent over a dishwasher. Dolores, I deduced.

'Have you had to come far?' asked Joey, when we reached a large square landing with rooms off. 'There's a loo there, by the way.'

'OK,' I said. 'Just a couple of miles, actually. It's an easy bus journey.' Dylan had told me never to drive to the house, and given me extra for taxis.

The landing wallpaper had a pink-jungle motif and I was trying to work out how I felt about it when a figure appeared silhouetted in the farthest doorway.

'Join me in a glass of red, Marie?' said Suzie. 'Joey, love, could you organise those?'

'Are you all right with wine?' he asked me, handing back my bag. 'It is only ten fifteen.'

Suzie groaned. 'Christ, the young are boring. Since when has it been a crime to drink in the morning?'

'I hate to be boring too,' I told her, my eyes taking in the opulence and chaos of the L-shaped room I'd walked into. A grand piano? 'But I'd love a coffee, please. Milk, no sugar. Thank you.'

'Same for you, Suze?' asked Joey.

'Yes, yes, coffee.' She flicked him away, then took my free hand and led me to a green velvet sofa. 'I'll have a dash of something in mine!' she called out. 'Now, sit yourself down, Marie, and we'll get to know one another.'

I dropped my bag and sank into the sofa, while Suzie sat straight-backed on the piano stool. She was slim, very, and had the deportment of a ballerina. Some of her thick blonde-grey hair was pulled back in a scrunchie and the rest hung to her shoulders. I could see her brother's mouth and dark-blue eyes, but her nose was more retroussé. She was barefoot and dressed in a snug, long-sleeved grey tunic top, with black leggings. Her décor may have been flamboyant but her wardrobe wasn't.

'Do you play?' I asked, nodding at the piano.

'Got to grade eight, would you believe. Now I just play my old favourites. Bob Dylan, the Eagles…'

'I do envy people who can play an instrument,' I told her.

'I should have thanked my mother for all those years of tortuous lessons, but I could never let go of the resentment.' She laughed, revealing perfect white teeth. 'Now, tell me about yourself, Marie.'

'Well,' I said – this bit I'd prepared – 'I used to be a freelance journalist for several women's magazines, and then, out of the blue, one actress I'd done an interview with got in touch asking if I'd be interested in helping get her mess of an autobiography into shape. I said yes, and it sold well, and I got an agent who found me lots of similar work, mainly for TV and film stars. I'm winding it down now, though, and this will probably be my final book.' The last thing I needed was Suzie recommending me. 'My partner and I are hoping to move to Wales and live the rural life.'

'Christ, won't you find that tedious?'

'Oh, far from it. He has family near Bethesda and, well, we love it up there. The scenery, the walks. We're still mulling it over, though.' How lovely it sounded. I almost wished it were true.

'You know, I was in a commune in Mid Wales, back in the day. I was on a break, as they say, from my boyfriend, who was on a world concert tour.'

'Really?'

She smiled. 'More later, perhaps. Anyway, lots of sheep shit is my overriding memory. And boiling saucepans of water for a bath, ice on the insides of the windows, blocked toilets. Cats with fleas and chickens that got eaten by foxes. And the girls always being the ones to cook and wash up, while the chaps waited patiently for us to finish so they could have sex with us. If they'd run out of things to say about Marx, they didn't always wait.' She shook her head at me. 'Best bloody days of my life.'

'Oh!' I said, laughing.

I reached into my bag for a notepad. If she was going to tell me more, I ought to write it down. Or did I really need to, since there wouldn't actually be a memoir? Or would there? This really was the most confusing of jobs.

'Ah, Joey,' Suzie said, looking a bit misty-eyed. Still back in Wales, perhaps. 'Now which coffee has the booze in?'

By the time I'd put the notepad back and taken my mug from Joey, Suzie had moved on to the amazing rabbit Dolores had bought from the local butcher.

'You know, darling Norman could be Oxford's last family butcher. Oh, ha ha, that reminds me of the old Spike Milligan joke about the man who walks into a family butcher and says–'

'How much to do mine?' said Joey.

Suzie tutted and tapped his arm. 'Always spoiling my punchlines.'

'It's because I know them so well. Shall I ruin the accordion joke too?'

Interesting, I thought. Not exactly a boss and employee relationship. I hadn't wanted to interrupt the banter by saying it might have been Bill Bryson, not Spike Milligan.

Suzie placed her untouched coffee on a side table and leapt up. 'Let me give you a tour, Marie.'

'Oh right. OK.' I took a few sips of the very hot drink and placed my mug next to hers.

'And I have a lawn to mow,' said Joey. 'Shall I tell Dolores there'll be one more for lunch?'

'Would you like to join us?' Suzie asked me. 'We eat at half twelve.'

'That would be lovely, thank you.'

'Anything you don't eat?' asked Joey.

Offal came to mind, but what were the chances? 'Nope.'

'Cool. See you at lunch.

'Come along,' said Suzie, 'let's begin with the roof terrace.' Out on the landing, she stopped and grabbed my arm. 'Our coffees! Would you mind fetching them?'

'Of course not.'

The staircase to the attic brought us out onto another landing with three doors off it. First she showed me the room at the front, which had sloping walls and was a cross between a walk-in wardrobe and a library. 'The clothes are mine, the books are Pete's.'

'Pete?' I asked.

'My ex. People thought he treated me badly, but he really didn't. We just didn't marry, that's all. We were young and idealistic, and to be honest, Pete's been very generous over the decades. One never really knows what goes on in others' relationships. Are you in one, Marie?'

I paused, expecting her to suddenly remember. 'Yes,' was all I said. No point in mentioning the move to Wales again. 'And what was your ex's name?'

'Pete DuBarry. I expect you've heard of him?'

'I'm not sure. What does he do?'

'He's in a band.'

'Ah,' I said. 'Still? Which one?'

'Currently, Random Angels. They're an indie band. West Coast neo-psychedelic rock they call it. They're quite big, although they haven't been around that long. Just kids, really. I was backstage recently and heard them calling Pete "Band Dad". I tell him it's affectionate but he hates it. Before that he was with The Floors.'

'The Floors, wow.' They'd been Britain's version of The Doors, but without a cool name based on an Aldous Huxley book, or a pretty-boy vocalist. 'Didn't the singer die in a car accident?'

'Yes and no.' She leaned in towards me and lowered her voice. 'More of a drugs accident inside a car?'

'Right.'

'The band fell apart after that, but Pete's been lucky. For one, he's a brilliant lead guitarist, and they're hard to find. And secondly, he's still got his hair. Dyes it, of course. But a rock star with hair can go on into his dotage and still get girls throwing knickers at him. Even with a face like a bag of walnuts.'

'Yes, I can think of a few.'

I made a mental note for Dylan: S still very much in touch with P.

The middle door off the landing was to a Jack-and-Jill en suite that could also be entered through the rear room we were now in. I realised that the house lay roughly south to north. Where the first-floor drawing room had been south-facing and filled with light, this north-facing attic room, at the back of the house, was dimmer but in quite a serene way. It had in it two modern armchairs and a futon, presumably for guests to sleep on. There was a lot less going on here, decoratively, than in the rest of the house, and I spotted a couple of novels on the coffee table, one with a bookmark in it. An arched floor lamp hung over things. It felt like the perfect hideaway to read in.

'You'll often find Dolores up here,' said Suzie. 'When she's not working her magic in the kitchen.' Suzie handed me her mug and when she pushed open the French doors, more light came in the room. 'After you,' she said.

We stepped out onto what she'd referred to as a terrace, but what I'd have called a very small and frightening balcony. We were officially in the sky, with only an ornate iron railing between us and it. I stopped in my tracks. Who built it, and how? I wondered. Was it being held up by some flimsy flying buttress? And where had my knees gone?

'Ooh, steady,' said Suzie, catching my elbow and taking the mugs off me. 'Don't like heights?'

I remembered the London Eye trip not bothering me. Well, not for height reasons, but I stopped my mind going there. I'd even enjoyed the Shard. 'It was just unexpected,' I told her. 'I'm fine now, honestly.'

I lowered myself onto a cushioned chair, thinking only of what was between my feet and the ground, or rather what wasn't. 'How gorgeous it is up here,' I managed.

'Yes, I'm a very lucky girl. Although… no, I mustn't. It'll make me come across as spoiled, or entitled, and I'm really not.'

'I'm sure you're not. Go on…'

'I was going to say, given my time again, I'd have insisted we bought on the other side of the road. Then we'd have had a fabulous south-facing view of the city from the attic terrace – the dreaming spires of the colleges, Shotover Park to the east, Boars Hill to the south and Wytham Woods to the west…'

'Instead of…?' I asked, peering into the distance. 'Oh. Is that the orange of Kidlington Sainsbury's?'

'Probably,' she sighed. 'I blame Pete. Another thirty thousand and we could have bought number seven over the road. My husband was always tight with money, and I can see now that it might have been a motivation for not marrying me. It was pretty much his only flaw, though. Well, apart from his infidelity when touring.'

'That must have been hard for you?'

'Let's just say, while the cat was away…' She smiled slightly wickedly at me. 'Different times, Marie.'

Was that where I'd gone wrong with Greg? A bit of tit for tat and we might still have been living together.

Suzie sat staring over the treetops, drinking her coffee, miles away. After one sip of mine, I realised I had the laced one. It was very nice. On top of that, five or six gulps in, I lost all fear of the balcony. I relaxed into my chair and watched Suzie smile to herself, and then frown and purse her lips, then smile again, her eyes joining in. What was she remembering?

The lawnmower roaring into action seemed to shake her from those thoughts and suddenly she was on her feet again. 'Right,' she said. 'Onwards and upwards!'

'You're not taking me to the moon?' I asked and she laughed.

I quickly drained my cup – goodness, she was hard to keep up with – and made my way back to terra firma.

Out on the landing, Suzie clasped my hand. 'You know, Marie,' she said, 'I think you're going to be good for me.'

I guessed that meant I had the job.

* * *

For a plain-old-Monday lunch, Dolores produced an impressive range of dishes for us to dig into. A couscous salad covered in fresh herbs, chicken kebabs and lamb koftas on flatbread. She hailed from Manchester, I discovered, but had left home at the first opportunity and gone to sea.

'Luxury yacht charters,' she told me, fiddling with an interesting-looking charm bracelet. I wondered if she'd collected charms from around the world. 'I reached the giddy heights of chief steward. But after one harrowing charter when the chef flounced off and left us in the lurch, I stepped in and that was it. I'd found my passion, aged twenty-three. Did a cookery course, then went back to sea as a chef.'

'Where she had a *whale* of a time,' said Joey.

'Ha ha,' said Suzie, pointing her fork at him. 'Very good.'

'And not just in the kitchen, eh, Dolores?' he added.

'Well, you know,' she said. 'You squeeze a dozen twenty-somethings into cramped quarters, then throw in off-duty booze and a hot tub.'

'We get the picture, Dol,' said Joey. 'Although I'm trying *really* hard not to.' He pulled a face and had a napkin thrown at him.

Dolores was quite tall – around five-eight or nine – and had cropped fair hair. Practical for a cook, no doubt. She had a pretty, round face and blue eyes, and could easily have been Joey's sister.

'When did you give it up?' I asked.

'I was thirty-two and I realised how completely knackering all-day cooking was. Plus what tyrants the captains were, and what spoiled and bratty children the young staff had become. The guests, on the whole, were lovely.'

'It sounds like this place,' said Suzie.

'Thank you,' I said with a bow, and they laughed. What a jolly lot they were, but was this all for my benefit? When we'd finished our melon and ginger sorbets and a pot of tea was being poured into pretty cups, I said, 'So, what's the accordion joke?'

Suzie, who'd been beginning to droop, rallied and announced she'd do the honours. 'OK. So… what's the difference between an onion and an accordion?'

'I don't know,' I said, 'what *is* the difference between an onion and an accordion?'

She was already giggling. 'Nobody cries when you cut up an onion! No, wait…'

Joey groaned. 'Accordion, Suze. Nobody cries when you cut up an accordion.'

I wanted to join in the laughter but could see Suzie was hurt, despite the smile. 'I love the accordion,' I told them. I actually did.

'Me too,' said Suzie. 'Brian Jones on *Back Street Girl*. Fabulous.'

'Who?' asked Joey.

I knew who Brian Jones was, but not the song.

'Let's play it!' Suzie said, silently clapping. 'Joey, could you find the LP?'

'Sure. Which one?'

'Oh… um,' said Suzie, but Joey was already looking it up on his phone.

'The Rolling Stones,' he said. 'My nan's favourite.' He laughed then went and looked through a row of actual vinyl records I hadn't even noticed and pulled one out. Taking it from its sleeve, he then held it between his palms, like an old hand. After blowing dust off, he placed it on the turntable of a record player and moved the needle to the right spot. After a sweet bit of acoustic guitar, and Mick Jaggar's unusually gentle vocals, in came the accordion.

'Aah… wonderful,' said Suzie, swaying. 'It's a waltz. Listen… *dah*, dah, dah, *dah*, dah, dah…' And then she was on her feet and twirling around the room. 'Joey,' she said, beckoning him over. 'You lead.'

And then somehow, before I knew it, I was up and dancing-cum-plodding with Dolores, going, 'One, two, three, one, two three,' in my head – those decades of watching *Strictly* finally proving useful.

Once we'd all calmed down and were finishing our teas, Suzie began looking around the room, anxiously. 'Does anyone know where the treadle sewing machine is?'

Joey frowned and shook his head. 'I don't remember there being one, Suzie. Not since I've been here.'

'But…' she said.

'Dolores?' asked Joey. 'Have you seen it? You tend to wander around more than me. Top floor?'

Dolores looked at him but didn't answer.

'Hang on…' he said, 'just googling to see what they look like.'

'It was Granny T's,' said Suzie. 'She made me a pair of bell-bottoms on it. Rather slowly, I recall. By the time she'd finished, the world had moved on to flares.'

'Oh, right,' said Joey, showing his phone to Dolores. 'Nope. Think I would have noticed one of those.'

'How very odd,' said Suzie. She raised a hand and yawned behind it.

'Time for your nap?' asked Joey.

She gave him a withering look. 'Toddlers and old people nap. I take a siesta.' She turned my way. 'Come with me, Marie?'

Not to nap, I hoped. 'Of course,' I told her.

FOUR

At half six, Emily, Mike and I met up in the office.

'So how was your first day?' asked Mike.

'Well…' I described my arrival, the truly amazing house, the three occupants, the banter, the lunch, the dancing, and Suzie's anecdotes. 'Around two o'clock,' I told them, 'Suzie needed a nap. She insisted I accompany her to her bedroom, which is next to the drawing room on the first floor. Believe it or not, it was only then that the book came up. I'd almost forgotten that was why I was there. Anyway, she said could we start on it for real tomorrow at ten thirty, and I said of course, and then she got me to pass her the pill organiser from her dressing table because she always took a yellow one before her siesta.'

'Is she on a lot of medication?' asked Mike.

'I counted eleven. A day. Is that a lot?'

'My gran's eighty-eight,' said Emily, 'and got, like, everything wrong with her, and she's only on five a day.'

'Speaking of age,' I said, 'how old did you think Dylan was?' I'd found it hard to put an age to either sibling.

Emily pulled a face. 'Dunno. I can't really do old-age pensioners.'

'Fair enough.' I'd seen Dylan a second time, when he'd turned up with the laptop and counterfeit items. I still had no idea what he did for a living, or even his and Suzie's surname. And no name had appeared on his initial bank transfer to us. It was all part of his plan to stop me googling, of course. There were to be no careless references on my part, until Suzie herself had told me the information, or at least for the first couple of days.

'After that, my sister most likely won't remember what she's told you,' he'd said, 'and the others won't know, either.'

On my way back from Suzie's, I'd decided to remain uninformed for one more day. That meant not googling Pete and going down that route to Suzie. I'd told the others my decision. 'But you two can research all you want.'

'Don't worry, we will,' Emily had said.

'I'll call Dylan and give him a summary,' I told them now. 'Then I'll start recording Suzie from tomorrow and courier the tapes to him each day.'

'So,' said Emily, 'do you reckon Dylan's like some money-laundering dodgy businessman? And that's why he's able to get hold of fake ID stuff?'

Mike, who'd been quiet, sniggered. 'You know Edie's record on character assessment, Em. And besides, you're the psychic one. What do you sense?'

'Um…' Emily closed her eyes for a bit, then slowly opened them again. 'To be honest, the only bad vibe I'm getting is from – don't laugh – someone in yellow shoes?'

They both looked at me and I shook my head, then Mike said, 'Shit. Seth's got some.'

Emily grimaced. 'Oh God, I'm so sorry, Mike. It's all bollocks, you know, this psychic stuff, like Ben tells me just about every day.'

Mike stood and slipped his jacket back on. 'I've always hated them, and Seth knows it, but he still wears the fuckers. To be honest, I'm also getting bad vibes from him. Have been for a while. So well done for picking up on that, Em.'

'Thanks. I think. Is it all right if I go, Edie? Mum and Dad are with Flo and, you know…'

'What is it today?' I asked, shaking my head. '*Pride and Prejudice*?'

'Ha ha, think she's already done it.'

'No, no, that's good,' said Mike. 'Research shows that children can absorb and retain vast amounts at that age. It's like bilingually parented kids often don't speak at all until around three, then they're fluent in two languages.'

'So Flo might suddenly write a 19th-century classic?' I asked.

Emily giggled as she gathered her things. 'You know she said her first proper sentence yesterday. It was "Hands behind your back, sir!" Well, like, in Flo-speak. Her and her daddy play cops and baddies. She can't get enough. So sweet.'

* * *

After they'd gone, I called Dylan and told him about the warm welcome I'd received at the villa and that we'd start on the book project the next day.

'Did you know they don't always lock the front door?' I added.

'Unbelievable,' he said. 'But please don't lock it yourself, Edie. Just keep your eyes peeled.'

'I will. Oh yeah, and over lunch Suzie mentioned a treadle sewing machine. She thought there used to be one on the ground floor. Dolores and Joey swore they'd never seen it. Well, Joey did.'

'Um… I'm not sure I can picture it.'

'Oh, OK.' Because he couldn't recall what things looked like?

'That doesn't mean there wasn't one. I'll ask my daughter.'

I kept quiet about Suzie and Pete hanging out. Perhaps because of the way her face had lit up when she'd talked about him. Dylan disapproved of Pete, and most likely always would.

It made me think of Maeve and my ex, Billy. I'd instantly fallen in lust with him, in an alcohol-fuelled way, and then we'd grown closer and were as good as living together in the end. Billy had felt so good for me after years of loving arseholes. He was adoring and loyal. Biddable, but with just a hint of stubbornness. However, the first time Maeve met him, she'd taken me to one side and said, 'Not for you, Mum. Just get a spaniel.' And she'd never deviated from that opinion.

'You still there?' asked Dylan.

'Yes! Sorry.'

'I said I'll call you first thing tomorrow.'

'OK. Speak to you then.'

We ended the call and my mind drifted back to Billy. It had taken me many months to realise I hadn't wanted us to share either his or my house any longer. I'd wondered if we could just go on outings and walks. See exhibitions and open houses. Do lunches. After I'd proposed this to him, our calls and texts became fewer, while his mentions of his neighbour Naomi and their shared sourdough culture became more frequent. After they'd moved on to kefir, I'd answered Billy's calls less often and gradually drifted back to Greg.

Greg and I had always laughed a lot. I'd missed that. Since he'd moved out of my house – many years back – and into his cottage in Woodstock, we'd been very on–off. Now we were on, but since I still felt unable to totally trust him in the faithfulness department, I preferred to keep it casual, call the shots, and generally act like I wasn't too bothered. Obviously I was. Although approaching fifty, he was still pretty gorgeous. And, unfortunately, still teaching attractive under- and post-graduates.

'I've changed, Edie,' he'd tried to convince me. 'And so has the student culture. Christ, why would I respond to dick-pic requests from students, like one of my young colleagues does. It's debasing. Also, he's just been asked to leave.'

Because Greg hadn't reassured me *he* wasn't getting the requests, I'd cooled off for a week or two – basically sulked – then once he'd worked out why, he sent me a photo of what must have been the world's largest, saying "For your eyes only".

FIVE

'I grew up in an old rectory in a village in Norfolk,' said Suzie. We'd spent the first hour or so on her current house, her street, the neighbours, the Summertown shops and cafés, the dentists and doctors she used, and the beautiful canal and meadow walks on her doorstep.

'Sounds romantic,' I said. 'Rural Norfolk.'

'We were a quarter of a mile out of Norwich and on a bus route, so not entirely in the sticks. The rectory was Victorian and full of nooks and crannies, and had an ancient bell system to summon the servants. It was a big rambling place.'

'Sounds great.'

She nodded. 'It could be lonely, however. My mother was an actress, you see. She did a lot of repertory theatre, so was often away when the plays hit the road. Then it was just Daddy and me. I adored my father, oh and my nanny too. She was called Pauline. Am I going too fast, Marie?'

'Not at all.' I was jotting down the odd thing but mostly doodling. I pointed at the cassette player. 'I'm recording you?'

'Oh yes… anyway, Pauline was such fun. She loved board games and card games and swimming and tennis, and it felt like having an older fun-loving sister. Sadly, she only came part-time. Mostly, as I said, it was Daddy and me, and he was a quiet man. Spent a lot of time in his study.'

'What was your father's job?'

'He was a quantity surveyor. You know, Marie, to this day I have no idea what that entailed. I used to say it quite proudly to the girls at my boarding school in Oxford, and to the local boys we met in the park. "My father's a quantity surveyor." I'd add that he had his own firm and employed lots of people. That was what Mummy told me.'

Suzie stared into the middle distance for a while, then said, 'Shall we have a cocktail?'

'Um. Yes, why not?'

'Good girl!'

While Suzie rang Joey and ordered our drinks – telling him to surprise us – I took a good look around the drawing room, hoping to spot a photo of Dylan, so that I could bring him up. Suzie not mentioning him was beginning to feel odd. And there he was, on a shelf, alongside his sister and, presumably, their parents. I got up and took a closer look.

'Nice photo,' I said.

'Yes, isn't it? Our little nuclear family. That's my younger brother, Dylan. I think he was around fifteen, sixteen.'

'You look beautiful,' I told her.

'Bless you.'

'Your mother, too. Very glamorous. Is Dylan your only sibling?'

'He is. I love my brother, but he was always spoilt rotten by my mother. Dylan was a late and unexpected child for her, and having a new baby, combined with her advanced age, in actress terms, meant she had to give up touring and filming. I'd already been packed off to boarding school, aged eleven – mainly to make life easier for Daddy. Although I… no, let's leave that till later. Basically, even when I was around, all of Mummy's energy and attention – now that she no longer had audiences – had shifted to her baby boy.'

'Are your parents still alive?'

'No. Daddy went first. His heart. Then my mother and I grew closer, until her kidneys failed.'

'My father has dementia,' I said, fishing. I looked up to heaven and apologised to him. 'It's difficult.'

'I can imagine. We're lucky not to have that particular nightmare in the family. Not so far, touch wood.' She tapped the metal table the recorder was on.

I continued to walk around the room, looking at her pictures and photos.

'That's my niece when she was tiny,' she said. 'And that's Dylan, aged four.'

'He was very cute,' I told her.

'He certainly was. Everyone *adored* little Dylan.'

'Do you see much of him?'

'Not really. In fact, thinking about it, he hasn't visited for months!'

According to Dylan it had been the previous week. I wanted to ask how they got on, but didn't feel I could whilst recording. 'What does he do?' I said instead.

Joey arrived and placed a tray on the round Moroccan-style mosaic table between us. The drinks looked inviting, as did the two bowls of nuts. It was coming up to midday and I was definitely peckish.

'Remind me, Joey,' said Suzie. 'What is it Dylan does these days?'

'He's still running a top London restaurant, my love. And another in Norfolk. Marie, make sure you have some nibbles with Dolores's Molotov.'

'That strong, eh?'

'And some.'

'Cheers,' I said to Suzie, lifting my glass.

'Eye contact!' she insisted, raising hers. 'We don't want seven years' bad sex!'

* * *

Suzie's siesta, following a relatively subdued lunch, provided an opportunity to wander around the house, ostensibly looking for somewhere to set up my laptop. I took in all the *objets d'art* and paintings and rugs, to the best of my ability. It was a mix of styles and eras, and if my family hadn't been filling my house, I'd have happily taken it all home to look after. Clearly, making a mental inventory of it all wasn't doable. I wanted to take photos, but Dylan had told me not to, and what if he had someone monitoring the phone and computer he'd given me?

Back on the ground floor I put my laptop bag on the dining table and went to check out the garden. It was luxuriant, of course, and had several paths that meandered around small ponds, under trellised arches, past mirrors, statues and a curly-iron bench. A month hence there'd probably be lush foliage and an abundance of colour and I quite hoped I might be there to see it.

Back indoors and feeling a bit devil-may-care regarding Dylan – thanks to that cocktail and a small wine with lunch – I opened my laptop and began searching.

Apparently, Suzie DuBarry wasn't famous or interesting enough for a Wikipedia page, and no matter how many times I demanded a date of birth, Google didn't come up with one. There were only a couple of seventies and early-eighties images online of Suzie with Pete when they were together. Perhaps a first partner became less interesting to journalists once newer ones came along. They'd made an attractive couple, that was for sure, with their thick long hair and clothes that managed to flow and also be skintight.

I then found a handful of newspaper stories, mostly about her political and animal activism – climate change, fox hunting, hare coursing, farm conditions, and so on. In one quote from Suzie, she'd said, "Veganism is the only way forward." Maybe with the odd rabbit thrown in?

She'd marched in London against the Iraq invasion, and she'd made a speech against Brexit in Oxford's Bonn Square. Someone had uploaded a phone video of it on YouTube that had received nineteen views.

Suzie didn't seem to have a website, and she'd stopped tweeting in 2015. She hadn't posted very often before that, mainly retweets about upcoming demos. I couldn't find her on Instagram or Facebook.

Pete was a very different story, and following the millions of performances and recordings I'd whizzed past, I learned that seventy-eight-year-old Pete had had two proper marriages after Suzie and produced three children during each, and that he currently had four grandchildren.

In the latest photos with Random Angels, I could just about see the young handsome Pete in him, the guy I'd spotted wearing a silver catsuit in the photo next to Suzie's pills. He'd last divorced in 2023 and seemed not to have married since. It made me wonder how Suzie had felt about all those children, when she and Pete hadn't been able to conceive.

Since I still didn't have Dylan's surname, I typed in "Dylan restaurant London Norfolk" and his picture appeared halfway down page one. I read that Dylan McCrimmon was married to Fabienne McCrimmon – his business partner – and that his one daughter, Chloe, also worked in the restaurants. Again no Wiki page, but reviews for his two French-inspired restaurants, both called Fabienne, were impressive. I looked at a dozen or so Google images of him, with and without his family members and other staff, and checked out the food they dished up.

When Suzie emerged just after three, I joined her in the drawing room. Joey brought us tea and biscuits and reminded Suzie that she had a garden party to attend at six thirty.

She grimaced. 'At the Forsters'?'

'I'm afraid so,' he said.

'Can't I just…'

'Be under the weather again? That would make it three times in a row, Suze. Tell you what, I could put off Lily and come with you?'

'Would you, sweetie? That might make them slightly more bearable.'

'Sorry to be nosy,' I interjected, eyebrows raised, 'but what's wrong with the Forsters?'

'Fascists,' said Suzie.

Joey pulled a face at me. 'She means they voted for Brexit. You have to let it go, Suze. That was so long ago.'

Suzie looked bewildered. 'Surely it was only…' she said, shaking her head. 'Isn't there a joke about time… now let me… OK, got it. Why shouldn't you tell your watch a secret?'

'Because–' began Joey, until I nudged him to stop.

'I don't know,' I said. 'Why shouldn't I tell my watch a secret?' I felt a Christmas-cracker joke coming up.

'Because,' she said with a big white smile, 'time will tell!'

* * *

I got home just after five, and was pleased to see Jack in the kitchen.

'Hey, what have you been up to?' he asked.

'How long have you got?'

He looked over at the kids glued to the TV, then lifted the saucepan's lid to check its gurgling contents. 'Fifteen minutes?'

'Great.'

Jack Bevington and I had worked together on my first big case, when he'd been a one-man agency and I'd been a one-woman one, training young Emily. He'd then got together with Maeve and they'd moved to Brighton. I felt sure Jack would have jumped at the chance to get back into investigating, but there wasn't enough money in Fox Wilder's coffers for another part-time employee, and then there were Maeve's feelings to consider. Also, Jack *had* buggered off abroad with no word, mid-investigation, albeit to protect me and my family. But still.

'The garden?' I suggested.

'OK. Fancy a glass of wine?' he asked, switching off the hotplate. 'I bought a nice sauvignon blanc.'

Of course he had. I was so torn with Jack, half of me wanting him to get back with Maeve, half of me wanting him to find someone lovely and be happy. Not that my daughter wasn't lovely, but too much had been said and done during her months of post-natal depression – after Betty was born – that probably couldn't be unsaid or undone. I'd spent a lot of time in Brighton helping out and had been a witness to it all.

I poured the wine while Jack got two chairs out of the packed shed, then went back for the small table. I put a few nachos in a bowl without the kids seeing, then sat and took in the last of the day's sun.

My garden was so dull and messy, I decided, compared to Suzie's. The three used-and-rolled-up Pampers weren't helping. Neither were the Nerf guns, the ugly yellow sandpit with crocodile lid that was never on it, the broken trike and the trampled-on flower beds. Then there were the abandoned bits of food. I'd sometimes wished that Maeve's dog, Bear – the best Hoover ever – had moved here with them. Instead, Maeve and Jack had come to an informal arrangement with their new tenants. For a reduced rent, they were to take on the dog, temporarily, and the elderly top-floor lodger – presumably, for as long as she lasted.

'So, how's the job going?' I asked Jack.

He was working in a city-centre pub, on the food side. Most, but not all, of his shifts were in the evenings, which meant he could look after Betty during the day and collect Alfie from school. I tended to step in if he or Maeve were tied up.

'Work's not bad,' he said. 'Actually, I'm quite enjoying it. They're a really nice bunch.'

I detected a blush and raised an eyebrow at him. 'Any one nice person in particular?'

Jack was good-looking and personable. He also played guitar and sang his own songs, occasionally in the pub, and was a devoted dad. In other words, a catch. According to Maeve, who'd been in his pub for a drink just once, the female staff had been 'flirting their teenage arses off' with him.

'No,' he said, laughing. 'Too soon. Anyway, less of me. How's this odd new case going?'

'Er, oddly?'

I was telling him all about it when Maeve arrived home and stuck her head out of the door. 'Hi,' she said. 'Am I interrupting something?'

'No,' said Jack, jumping up to get another chair.

'How was your day?' I asked her.

Maeve had decided not to return to Oxford University when the studying bug hit her again, but rather, to go vocational and do a taught MSc in Accountancy and Finance at Brookes Uni, up in Headington. I, like others, had been quite shocked on hearing the news.

'Thing is,' she'd said when still considering it, 'I can't spend my life deconstructing Da Vinci in the Bodleian, or faffing around with bacon baps like I was in Brighton. I mean, my inheritance isn't going to last forever and I'm a single parent now and need to plan and be sensible and that means having a decent, regular income.' I'd got quite choked up, hearing her talking so adultly, but then she'd said, 'I'm just not like you, Mum,' and ruined it.

Maeve sat on the chair Jack had opened for her and sighed. 'The course is quite hard, to be honest. Wish I'd taken maths more seriously at school.'

'You're not going to fail?' I asked, a little too strongly. I knew how much the fees had been.

'I might.' She shrugged and looked forlorn, but then burst out laughing. 'Mum, your face! I don't fail at things, remember?' She gave me a hug and looked over at Jack. 'Only relationships, but I think that's genetic.'

'Kid alert,' said Jack, as Alfie wandered across the patio and asked what genetic meant.

'It means it's in your body, in your genes,' said Maeve, taking her arm from me and cuddling Alfie.

'Like D and A?' asked my grandson, the genius.

'That's right,' said Maeve. 'DNA. We all get half of our genes from our mother and half from our father. And genes give us things like whether we're good at sport, or music, or if we have big ears. Our genes can also make us not behave too well sometimes.'

'I think that's debatable,' said Jack.

Alfie helped himself to a nacho. 'So,' he said as he crunched, 'are half my genes from Jesus? Cos if they are, I think they're all bad, else why doesn't he want to see me?'

'Oh, honey,' said Maeve. 'It's not that he doesn't want to see you, it's just that your real dad doesn't know about you, and I can't find him to tell him he's got a brilliant little boy.'

Alfie nodded, but was that a small tear in his eye? I had to go before I cried too. I'd told Maeve at the time that I thought six was too young to tell Alfie about Jesus – aka Heyzoos – a gap-year fling on the other side of the world. But had she listened?

'Just popping to the loo,' I said.

In the kitchen I found Betty on the floor playing with the spilled contents of her mum's bag: one opened-up lipstick, one open mascara, one eye pencil with the top off, purse, pens and two condoms. I shoved the latter items back in the rucksack before Jack saw them, then took a wriggling and wailing Betty upstairs to the bathroom to clean her red-and-black face. As she pounded my aching arm and said she hated me, my thoughts turned to the villa. Was Suzie foxtrotting to the Kinks? Or had she and Joey gone to the party? Had there ever been a treadle sewing machine? And who was Lily?

I delivered a pink-faced Betty to her parents and said sorry but I had to go and meet Mike at the office.

* * *

Once on the Cowley Road, I picked up a warm falafel wrap, a coffee and four mini bottles of white that would fit in the office's mini fridge. Then, over the next three hours, I discovered the appeal of *The Real Housewives* franchise. As I sat at my desk and watched episode after episode – wondering where exactly Orange County was and why décor was so dire back in 2008 – I was completely absorbed and forgot about the wine.

Back at home all was quiet, and so I went straight to bed, only to wake up from a nightmare, heart thumping, a couple of hours later. In the dream I'd been walking around my house but it was all Orange County dark wood and shag-pile carpets. Stopping by a mirror I'd seen Betty's face covered in badly applied make-up. When I tried to find a bathroom to wash it off, I opened a door onto a tiny balcony, where I promptly tripped and found myself falling, and falling…

When I was little, someone had told me that if you fall like that in a dream and actually land, then you die in real life. But how, I'd wondered, would the dead person report their dream? When I'd asked my policeman dad, he'd told me I'd make a great detective.

SIX

Suzie's front door was unlocked again, but I still tapped on the glass panel and said, 'Yoo-hoo!' as I entered. No response came back. There was a white van on the drive, so I assumed something, somewhere was being fixed or painted.

I sat on the hall chair and switched to my indoor shoes, then when I went to lean on the arm it wasn't there and I almost tipped over. I got up and took a look. Gone was the beautiful old art deco chair with its geometric back slats and jacquard-print seat, and in its place was one of the chunky wooden chairs that surrounded the kitchen table. This one had been painted lilac. I scanned the hall and couldn't see the original anywhere. The umbrella stand was there, in its usual place, and everything else seemed more or less the same.

'Joey! Tea's ready!' came an unfamiliar voice.

I wandered into the kitchen and found a petite young woman with braids carrying two mugs.

'There you go,' she said, placing one in front of Dolores, who had her head in her hands, elbows on the dining table. 'And here's two ibuprofen.'

Joey appeared from the garden and waved. 'Hi, Marie. Just the person I was hoping to see. Fancy a coffee?'

'Please. Instant's fine.'

'This is my girlfriend, Lily, by the way. Lily, Marie.'

We both said hello and I pulled out the chair next to Dolores. 'How are you?' I asked her.

'Not too bad,' she said, 'considering I got rat-arsed last night.'

'Oh? Some exciting event?'

Joey laughed heartily as he stirred milk into my mug.

Dolores gave him the middle finger. 'At least Scrabble takes some intelligence to play, unlike football.'

'Shows how little you know about the game, Dol. My team members and I do a hell of a lot of planning. Tactics, formations and the like.'

'Only because you've got a crap trainer, captain, whatever. And don't call me Dol.' She shook her head and turned back to me. 'It was the final of the Scrabble tournament I take part in every year.'

'She came second,' said Joey.

'That reminds me of the joke about the chicken and the egg having sex,' said Suzie, swanning in from the garden in a chic boiler suit. She put a bunch of herbs in a small jug, then sat at the head of the table. 'Morning, Marie.'

'Hi, Suzie.' I returned her smile. 'How are you?'

'I'm super, thanks. And very much looking forward to our session.'

Joey put my coffee on the table and sat opposite me, beside Lily. 'Got an invitation for you,' he said.

'What to?' I asked.

'My thirty-second birthday party!'

Dolores cleared her throat.

'OK, thirty-fifth,' said Joey, laughing. 'A week Saturday.' He put his hand on top of his girlfriend's. 'Lily's a fantastic party planner, so we thought we'd have a conflab once you arrived. Oh, it's to be held here, by the way.'

'I insisted,' said Suzie.

Lily put her hands together in prayer. '*Please* come, Marie. Joey's invited his entire football team and we need more women.'

'We'd also love your company,' said Joey, nudging Lily. 'And if you have any female friends who'd fancy it…'

'I might know someone,' I said, thinking Astrid could well be up for a footballer. 'Do you party plan professionally?' I asked Lily.

'That's the aim. Early days, though.'

'Is that your van out front?'

'It is. Bit of a wreck but it's good for ferrying party stuff around.'

'There'll be live music from Pete and his band,' chipped in Suzie. 'Bugger the neighbours!'

'Sounds great,' I told Joey. 'Is there a theme, or a dress code?'

He looked at Lily for a while, then said, 'How about a "come as your authentic self" theme?'

From across the table, both Joey and Lily held direct eye contact with me. Shit, I thought. Do they know?

'In that case,' said Suzie, 'I'm coming as a Norfolk dumpling!'

Joey shook his head in a baffled way, and Lily giggled. Dolores rubbed her temples.

'OK, Marie,' said Suzie, standing up. 'Let's leave them to discuss party food and I'll tell you all about boarding school.'

'Right you are.' I grabbed my heavy bag, my lighter handbag and my coffee and followed Suzie up the stairs.

'Want a hand?' called out Joey, too late.

The sun was dazzling us, so Suzie lowered a couple of cream-coloured Venetian blinds. Suddenly the room had a much cosier feel, with the vibrant mix of colours now muted.

'My best friends were Rowena and Caroline,' said Suzie, before I'd had time to press record. 'Ro and Caro. Ro's father was a Lincolnshire farmer and Caro's did something oil-related in Bahrain. Occasionally, when it was a short school holiday, Caro would spend it with one of us, rather than travel all that way. The first time she stayed with me, when we were both eleven, I took a pound note from Daddy's wallet and we went into Norwich on the bus without telling him. Mummy was touring, of course. Or perhaps she was on a film set. She sometimes had minor roles in things like the *Carry On* films.'

'That must have been fun for her?'

'She hated filming. Said she much preferred a living, breathing, farting audience.' Suzie chuckled. 'Mummy liked to shock.' She got up and paced around. 'That trip into Norwich was such fun. Shoplifting Biros and sweets and pale lipsticks from Woolworths, and trying on miniskirts in Chelsea Girl that we couldn't possibly buy and that were too big for us anyway. My father somehow found out, but he just laughed and said, "Thank heaven for boarding schools!" Caro said her father would have given her a jolly good hiding. I think she developed a bit of a crush on Daddy over the years… until, well…' Suzie took a deep breath and sat on the piano stool. 'Until it all came crashing down.' She turned and looked at me. 'But again, Marie, that's a story for another day.'

'OK,' I said, both disappointed and relieved.

'I liked English best,' she continued, 'and netball. And boarding in the dorms was so much nicer than living in a large house with an often-absent mother. I was a bit of a rule breaker, and of course that made me popular. And I told rude jokes Mummy had heard on tour.'

'Were you allowed out of school?' I asked. 'Unaccompanied?'

'Once we were thirteen, yes. We had chores every Saturday morning, then after lunch we were let loose on Oxford, until teatime.' Suzie smiled wistfully and went quiet for a while, her features turning more serious.

'Are you all right?' I asked.

'Yes, yes. Just… happy days, you know?' She reached for her phone and tapped it. 'Joey, sweetie, I think a vodka and cranberry juice might be called for… and add something sweet. One for you, Marie?'

Oh, what the hell, I thought, giving her a thumbs up. When the door immediately opened, I spun around.

'Would you like all the trimmings, Suze?' asked Joey, the phone still at his ear.

'Oh, ha ha,' she said, hanging up. 'Such a prankster. Yes, of course we would.'

* * *

We had a quiet lunch with no Joey or Lily, who'd gone off in the van to buy party provisions. Or sell the art deco chair. Then, while Suzie slept, I made my way up to the attic and stretched out on the futon, two cushions under my buzzing head.

There was a lot to unpack. Joey's birthday party and what to wear and who to bring. The life or boarding-school catastrophe hinted at by Suzie. Joey, right outside the drawing room. Listening in? The missing chair and Lily's convenient van. Then there was Astrid. If I brought her to the party, would she put her foot in it, either unthinkingly or provocatively? Probably not worth the risk. I'd ask Emily to arrange childcare, so she could come along. What, I wondered, might Greg be doing that evening… or even this evening. It would be nice to see him… should I call and suggest…

I woke up and panicked, not knowing where I was at first. My phone said ten to three. Good. Time for a coffee before round two.

* * *

Almost an hour later, Suzie joined me in the drawing room. She sat on the green velvet sofa and nodded for me to press record.

'In November, when I was fifteen and studying for O-levels, I was called to the school office, where my mother was on the line. She needed me to come home straight away, she said. Daddy was driving down to Oxford to pick me up, so I was to pack absolutely everything and be ready at the gate in three and a half hours.'

'Crikey,' I said. 'Why?'

'I asked myself that question, over and over, as I walked back to the dorm. Without access to a phone to ring Mummy back, I had no option but to wait for Daddy to explain. When he arrived, he drove us into Oxford city centre and we went to the Cadena Café in Cornmarket Street. They served us boiled eggs and brown and white bread, followed by cream cakes. Best of all, though, was the small orchestra playing in the corner. It felt like the height of sophistication, and to be there with Daddy made it very special.'

'Sounds wonderful.'

Suzie's smile faded. 'Unfortunately, the magical spell was broken by one sentence. "Your mother's going to have a baby," said my father, and instead of looking happy, his expression was miserable. "She's feeling terribly unwell and keeps saying she needs her little girl at home, to comfort and help her." I instantly burst into tears and asked when I'd be able to go back to school, and Daddy patted my hand and said, "We'll see, darling." All I could think about were Ro and Caro and never seeing them again, and we had to leave the Cadena Café because I was sobbing so much.'

'Goodness, Suzie. How awful for you.'

'Yes. It was altogether a ghastly period. My parents were frosty with one another, Mummy grew bigger and bigger, and I loathed the grammar school I had to go to from the following September. They put me back a year so I could take my O-levels. However…' Suzie looked at me and smiled. 'It wasn't all bad. I made good friends, some of whom I'm still in touch with, and Norwich was quite fun for teenagers. All the big bands, or groups as we called them back then, came and played there. And with Mummy so caught up with her darling baby son, I actually had a lot of freedom. Then, when I was almost seventeen, The Floors did a gig in Dereham, and, once again, my life went on a different trajectory. I met Pete.'

'Gosh, you were so young.'

'Not really. Back then, girls were often jettisoned into a typing pool, aged sixteen, or they started nursing training. The options for girls were limited, you understand. Shorthand typist, shop assistant, teacher, nurse. I managed good O-level results, despite the distraction of Pete, but Mummy still insisted I did a shorthand and touch-typing course. After my breakup with Pete, it did come in useful. I had to temp for a year in bloody awful catty offices, while my solicitor fought for a fair division of assets. I actually did rather well, considering there were no children, and that we'd never actually been married.'

'Did you ever see Ro or Caro again?'

'No I didn't. Daddy promised me five pounds and a cinema trip if I stopped crying, and they just sort of fell out of my head!' She chuckled. 'Until recently that is… the memoir… makes you think back over everything, good and bad. Memories pop up and take you by surprise. People, places, emotions…'

Her phone screen suddenly lit up with a call. 'Joey,' she told me, answering it. She listened for a while. 'Wonderful!' she exclaimed. 'Oh, that is good news! Where is it now? … Excellent … Yes … Yes … See you at dinner, sweetie.'

She leaned back and sighed. 'It seems Joey was tackling the brambles behind the shed, when he spotted something made of metal and wood, all tangled up in them.'

'Not Granny T's sewing machine?'

'Can you believe it! Lord knows how it got there. Anyway, he and Lily have given it a good clean and it's waiting for me to decide where it's to go. Tell me, Marie, have I mentioned my early-teen puppy fat?'

'No?' I said, now getting used to Suzie's mercurial mind.

'My mother sent me to adult keep-fit classes in the hols, but the weight didn't shift. "My little Norfolk dumpling", she'd call me in front of Caro.' Suzie snorted. 'That was so Mummy. I think she might have been labelled a narcissist these days. Where do you stand on labels, Marie?'

I hesitated, not wanting to land myself in a Brexiteer-type category. 'I suppose they might be useful… sometimes?'

'Daddy had his faults, too,' she ploughed on. 'I very gradually learned from Mummy, once I was living back at home, that my father was a serial philanderer, who'd been having it off with my nanny, and who didn't in fact have his own large and successful firm. He *was* a quantity surveyor, but he'd had to leave job after job, and ended up freelancing. My mother's income had been keeping the family and home afloat, but when that source dried up, owing to her pregnancy, they could no longer afford the boarding school fees.'

'Oh,' I said, running out of responses. I wasn't sure I could take much more. On top of that, I was growing anxious about time and Oxford's rush hour. A courier came to my house at six each day to pick up the cassette tapes and I had no idea how to contact them to say I'd be late.

'Poor Daddy,' she continued. 'It must have killed him to have taken me out of school.'

'I'm sorry you had to go through that,' I said, feeling Suzie had let her father off lightly. I took the cassette out of the machine, then gathered my bags. 'Sorry I have to dash,' I told her. 'Same time tomorrow?'

'Oh,' said Suzie. 'I believe I have a doctor's appointment. Would you mind if we skipped a day?'

'No problem,' I told her. 'It'll give me time to write up the recordings.'

Suzie walked me to the door and gave me an unexpected hug. 'I'm finding this terribly therapeutic, Marie.'

'Good.'

'See you tomorrow,' she said, pulling back.

'You mean Friday?'

'I... yes, of course. Because... tomorrow I have an appointment?'

'Shall we write it down?' I suggested.

* * *

While sitting on the lilac chair to change my shoes, I heard a heated conversation coming from Dolores's room across the hall. I could pick out the voices of Dolores and someone else, but not what they were saying. Dolores was loud, but the other voice was quieter, and male. He said something else and I realised it was Joey.

'It just isn't right!' shouted Dolores, and rather than be found listening in the hall, I decided to go to the kitchen, thinking I'd get a glass of water and eke it out until someone left that room.

I rounded the corner and there, beside the dining table, stood the treadle sewing machine. It was lovely. Quite dainty and made of dark glossy wood. All of its ornate metal parts were beautifully shiny too. I went closer and inspected... no bramble scratches... no damp and rotting patches... no rust. Either Joey and Lily had worked their socks off French polishing and Brasso-ing it earlier, or they'd bought back the original.

Having filled a glass with tap water, I leaned against the sink and listened out for movements. After a while I heard Dolores's door open, and then I heard it shut. And then another door closed. It had to be Joey's, because the big front door always thunked and rattled distinctively. I considered running the gauntlet to the front door, but then remembered a side passage to the left of the house. But when I went and checked it out, a locked gate blocked that route.

Back in the kitchen, I became aware of how peaceful, yet eerily surreal the place felt: the aroma of fresh thyme and mint wafting my way from a jug; birds chirruping through the open French doors; a manual lawnmower trundling along; and piano music floating down from Suzie's room. She sounded pretty good, and the song was really familiar. *It's All Over Now, Baby Blue*? Greg and I had once argued over whose version was the better, Bob Dylan's or Bryan Ferry's. Obviously, Bryan's is.

When it finally felt safe, I crept along the hallway to the front door, where another sound joined the others. It was Dolores crying.

SEVEN

The next day, the Fox Wilder team met in the office during Emily's lunch break and I told them about Suzie's childhood and the strange goings-on at the villa. I also mentioned Joey's birthday party.

'I've OKed it with Dylan, but didn't tell him they were practically begging for me to bring people along. I wasn't sure it would be a wise thing to do, or if you guys would even want to come.'

'I'm in,' said Mike. 'You could introduce me as a general handyman?'

'I could. How about you, Emily?'

'You're asking if I want to go to a party in a big posh house that Random Angels might be at? Ha ha, I think it's a yes from me too.'

'Good. We'll have to come up with a persona for you.'

'Cool,' said Emily. 'How about intuitive psychic astrologer?'

'That's a profession?' asked Mike. 'And how much do you know about Virgo in Uranus – 'scuse my French – and all that?'

'I do know that's not how you say *Ur*anus, Mike. I'll be all right. I've got two days to learn it.'

Mike looked sceptical but Emily claimed to have a photographic memory, so I wasn't worried. 'Also…' I said, 'I, um…'

'What?' asked Emily.

'I was thinking of taking Astrid along to the pa–'

'No!' they both cried.

'Why not?'

'How about,' said Mike, making moves to leave, 'because she doesn't give a fuck?'

'There is that,' I said. 'But she's going through a rough time.'

'Aww,' said Emily. 'In that case…'

Mike growled and hooked his bag over one shoulder. At the door he grinned my way. 'A whole football team, you say?'

* * *

Later, I called for Astrid, and as we walked into town via the Botanic Garden, she reeled off a list of domestic grievances that included her elderly male neighbour hanging gigantic Y-fronts out to dry. 'It's not funny, Edie. They're literally grey.'

In the restaurant area at the top of the Westgate, we found a free outdoor table with a view of the city, where Astrid fretted over the prospect of having to find decently paid work.

'What did you do before the ceramics business?' I asked. I couldn't remember her ever saying.

'Club work mainly. In London.'

'Really? What kind of clubs?'

Astrid almost smiled. 'The ones that paid the most, or rather the ones where the punters did, if you get my meaning. What? Please close your mouth, Edie. I tell you, it was more exciting than shop work and far more lucrative.' She took a tissue from her bag and mopped up the coffee I'd just spilt. 'So,' she said, 'you were going to tell me about this Suzie woman. What exactly have you been asked to do? Write a book?'

'Well…' I said, recovering.

I started at the beginning with Dylan coming to see me. The good thing about Astrid was that, given an interesting subject, she'd listen wholeheartedly. Betty's chickenpox or British politics and she'd be checking her phone within seconds. I told her about the upcoming party and then I somehow invited her.

'Mike will pose as a general handyman and gardener, and Emily will be a psychic astrologer.'

'Mm,' she said, now only half listening. 'This Dolores woman.'

'Yes?'

'What are the chances she's romantically involved with Joey?'

'Oh!' I said, a bit thrown. 'Not sure. I mean they do sleep across the hall from each other. On the other hand, there is Lily. Why?'

'Because he made her cry, and I'm sure it wasn't over a sewing machine.'

'I don't know if he made her cry, or if he was just there.'

'Personally, I've never shed tears over a man. You?'

'Rivers' worth. Maybe an entire ocean. I still sometimes…'

'Oh Lord.' She sighed. 'Not over Bloody Greg? Can't you just screw him and be happy with that? I mean, everything else in your life is uncertain and shambolic.'

'True,' I said, although she was hardly one to talk. At least I had a shower cubicle. 'So, are you coming to the party?'

Astrid said she'd think about it. I could see she was torn. She might have disliked people, but she loved bohemian posh. What, I wondered, if I offered her money?

'I thought you might be able to do a bit of flirting and digging,' I said, 'with the guys… Joey and his friends? Pete, if he's there. And Mike could do the same with the women. I'd pay you, if you like?'

'Would you?' she asked. 'Jonathan's being terribly generous but says he can't stretch to four-hundred-pound hair appointments in London.'

'Bloody hell, Astrid. What do they do for that?' Her hair was straight, shoulder-length and naturally blonde. It had never looked any different in the time I'd known her.

'Make me feel important?'

'But you're so good at doing that yourself!'

I laughed, alone, then for the second time ever I saw her cry. Well, her eyes reddened and she blinked a few times.

'I've found myself forced to shop at Aldi,' she whispered. 'Can you imagine?'

'Er, yeah. The whole world does. Aldi, Lidl…'

'When I asked the girl for prosecco, she led me to prosciutto. It's just too much, Edie.'

I wanted to get up and hug her better, then remembered there was real suffering going on in the world. 'Shall we get a bus back?' I asked to a completely blank response. 'They're big and you buy a ticket when you get on?'

'Ah,' she said, then waved her phone at me. 'Cab will be here in ten.'

I paid the bill and we made our way down to Castle Street to meet the driver. On the silent drive to the Cowley Road, where I was to be dropped off first, I kept seeing Astrid the stripper – men tucking tenners in her thong. Had it paid well? I wondered. Had she met lovely Jonathan that way? No, unlikely. I shook my head to dispel the images, then got out near home. Before closing the taxi door, I watched Astrid lean forward and ask to be taken to Aldi.

'I'll need you to wait while I shop,' she added.

'No!' I cried. 'Astrid, what's the point of that?' It was obviously taking her a while to grasp living on a budget. 'Look, I'll take you. Come on. We need some things, too.' We always did.

We actually went to Lidl, where Astrid found both prosecco and, in the middle aisle, a fantastic little black dress for £12.99.

'You could wear it to the party,' I joked, slightly cross I hadn't found it first. I could hardly buy one too.

EIGHT

On my arrival at Suzie's on Friday morning, she popped up from behind the Audi with a handful of weeds. 'Marie!' she cried. 'How lovely to see you! Why don't you get a coffee, and I'll meet you upstairs in two ticks.'

'OK.'

After changing my shoes, I made my way to the kitchen, where there were no signs of life. No Dolores, just a pile of dirty plates beside the sink, used pans on the cooker and a sticky floor. I prayed she hadn't left. No more yummy lunches was my first selfish thought, and probably my second too. Hopefully, Joey could cook. I hadn't had breakfast, that was the problem, so busy had I been making packed lunches for two picky eaters – 'Carrot sticks, yuck!' – and so on.

I made an instant coffee and hurried upstairs, hoping to have a quick nose around Suzie's drawing room. Looking down from the window, I saw she'd moved to a different spot. She was kneeling on a cushion, and beside her was a shallow basket filled with cuttings and weeds.

I quickly checked the landing to make sure Joey wasn't lurking, then did something I wasn't proud of, but Dylan wasn't paying me to sit around drinking cocktails. I turned the tiny key in the bureau-style desk and lowered the lid, my heart thumping wildly. If I'd been in a film there'd have been tense background music and cuts to Suzie mounting the stairs. I checked again. Still weeding.

The desk was a mess. Each small compartment was stuffed with leaflets, flyers and menus, and the large inlaid ink blotter was covered with pens and felt tips, old packets of mints, more leaflets, business cards, assorted keys, aspirin and a large number of ponytail hairbands. There were two old mobile phones and tangled-up chargers. I quickly shut the lid and went to the window. Suzie had moved along again and was jabbing the narrow border with a small fork. I thought I heard her singing.

Back at the desk I turned the key in the top drawer of three, where I found folders labelled "Insurance", "Utilities" and the unfortunate "Passwords etc.". I'd hoped to come across bank statements and a newly drawn-up will leaving everything to her carers, but perhaps the second drawer… It opened with the same key and was filled to the brim with press cuttings and studio photos of Suzie's mother. I delved down and found more of the same.

After checking on Suzie again, I went back to the bureau to look in the bottom drawer. The key wouldn't open that one and, what's more, it had a different, newer-looking keyhole. Lowering the desk lid again, I went through the six or seven keys but none were small enough, so I closed the bureau, locked everything, then peered into various decorative pots and bowls along the windowsill. No key. Damn. I looked around the room for anywhere else I might find paperwork, but saw nothing obvious.

My phone told me I'd arrived thirty minutes ago, so giving up on the search I hoisted one of the sash windows and called out, 'Suzie!' making her jump and cry out before looking up at me.

'Marie?' she said, raising herself with the aid of the Audi. 'Here already? I'll be with you in a sec.'

'I'll come down,' I told her. 'Want a coffee?'

'I'd love one!'

By the time Suzie had cleaned herself up and I'd reheated her coffee twice, it was approaching half eleven. When we finally sat down on either end of the green sofa, I pressed record.

'Right,' she said, brushing the last bits of garden from her leggings. 'I thought I'd talk about boarding school today. Is that OK?'

'Of course.' I wanted to hear more about the boys she and her friends had met in town, and about any eccentric teachers, or bizarre punishments.

'Where shall I begin?' she said, taking a deep breath. 'Well, my two best friends were Ro and Caro. Rowena and Caroline. Caroline's parents were in Bahrain. Something to do with oil. So, sometimes, during shorter holidays, she stayed with us.'

Suzie went on to tell me about her mother calling the school and telling her to pack all her belongings because her father would be picking her up. I let her recount it all again, thinking it would give Dylan added insight into his sister's memory issues. Give or take some details, her story was the same. She and her father had eaten boiled eggs and brown bread and butter, while the small orchestra played.

'When Daddy broke the news to me, about the baby,' she said, 'and that I wouldn't be able to return to school, I immediately burst into tears.'

The eggs and brown bread had my mind wandering to lunch, and whether or not Dolores would be making it. No lovely aromas were wafting their way towards us, as often happened around that time. When Suzie was finished, I decided, I'd ask her outright.

'I was completely distraught,' she was saying, her eyes now welling up. 'And then the most shameful thing happened.' She looked up at me.

'What?' I asked.

'I'd got myself into such a tizz that I vomited all over the white tablecloth.'

'Oh, no!'

'The waitresses were terribly nice. One folded the tablecloth over the ghastly mess and with the help of the clarinet player carried it away. Daddy's face was so red. He must have been blushing, rather than cross. Daddy didn't do angry. Then another waitress, called Irene, took me to the powder room and cleaned me up. She fetched me a Fox's Glacier Mint from her handbag, to take the nasty taste away. I remember thinking that I'd rather go home with Irene than back to my mother. Wasn't that awful of me?'

'Well…'

Suzie dabbed at her eyes with the back of her hand, straightened her posture and smiled at me. 'I've never touched a boiled egg since.'

'Understandably,' I said, appalled by the young Suzie's experience. Had she been too embarrassed to bring it up – so to speak – the other day? 'I always hate those inevitable bits of shell,' I added.

'Ugh, don't.'

'Speaking of food,' I ventured, 'I didn't see Dolores when I arrived. Is she here today?'

'Um… Dolores, Dolores,' she said, frowning. 'Yes. I mean, no. She's had to pop up to… home.'

'Manchester?'

'That's it!'

'So will there be any lunch?' I asked boldly and hungrily. 'I could always pop to the Summertown shops for sandwiches?'

'Oh, no need, Marie. I'm sure we have bread I can rustle up a sandwich with.'

I was thinking of her rock-hard jam tarts when the door flew open and Joey said, 'Ladies, are you OK with chicken nuggets and baked beans?' As freaked out as I was by his lurking presence, I wanted to kiss him.

NINE

On Saturday, Maeve took me to one side and asked if I could look after the kids while she went to view a couple of houses to rent. I agreed but felt strangely alarmed. Suddenly, all the pluses of having my family on site overwhelmed the negatives. In the time they'd been there, I'd grown closer to Alfie, my new best friend. He and I had done tours of three colleges together, and we'd climbed up the University Church tower, where we'd pointed at landmarks and to roughly where our house was. I'd also regularly taken him on the bus to the central library. He'd sat on the floor engrossed in children's history and science books, then we'd carried his maximum allowance home.

He was showing signs of his mother's intellectual curiosity, and when, a few weeks back, he and I had gone around Christ Church College and Cathedral, he'd been my tour guide. I'd asked how he knew so much and he'd said, 'YouTube, dummy!' and laughed.

Alfie was still cheeky, but he was also still extremely cute, what with the Spanish features he'd inherited from both Maeve and the absent Jesus. He was one of those children adults smile at, which was nice but also unnerving. I liked to think we'd all rammed the never-talk-to-strangers message home, but he was still small enough to be bundled into a vehicle and taken abroad. Hopefully, he'd never know how close he'd come to that as a three-year-old.

Another Alfie plus was that, unlike his sister, he didn't ignore me, attack me, or rat me out to his mum.

* * *

I decided to drive the kids to Blenheim Palace in Woodstock. All the way there, I prayed I wouldn't bump into Greg and a beautiful girl with the figure of Tinker Bell.

At the entrance to palace I bought a year-long family pass that Maeve could also use. Having toured the palace itself a few times, I knew it would be of interest to Alfie but not Betty. I'd bring him back alone sometime soon, I decided.

Once parked, we took the miniature open-air train – which Betty loved – to the walled garden, where we went around the butterfly house – in which Betty quickly grew bored – to the adventure playground – for which Betty was too small – then into the two-mile-long mini-yew-tree maze – which Alfie loved, until we lost track of him but could hear him calling and crying in the distance.

I lifted Betty to the safety of my arms and set off in what I felt was the right direction, calling out his name. But then Alfie went quiet, and for what felt like an hour, but which was probably three minutes, I convinced myself – knot in stomach, mildly hyperventilating – that my greatest fear had actually happened.

'Alfie!' I called again, hearing the panic in my voice. 'Alfie! Shout if you can hear me!'

Betty was trying to wriggle out of my arms but I desperately clung on, determined to go home with at least one child.

When, finally, we rounded yet another yew-tree bend to see a girl of twelve or so leading my red-eyed, shell-shocked grandson by the hand, I hid my tears, put Betty down, and gave him a grateful hug.

In the café, over hot chocolate, I rewrote history with Alfie, bigging him up for being so adventurous. 'And how clever you were to find us!' I said, hoping that would be the version he'd give his mum.

When Betty started saying, 'Want Mummy,' over and over, we finished our meal and after a bit of a wait caught the miniature train back in a rapidly dropping temperature that made Betty shiver and cry while refusing to let me cuddle her warm.

At four fifteen both kids were strapped into the car with the ice-cream cones they'd begged for. I started the engine and said, 'That was fun, wasn't it?'

'Yeah!' cried Alfie.

'Shall we come again?'

'Yeah!' cried Alfie.

'Betty?' I said to no response.

When I twisted the rear-view mirror, I saw she was asleep with her chin in her ice cream. Maeve's 'Absolutely *no* naps after three!' rang in my head and I reached back to tickle her awake. But then stopped. She looked peaceful and almost happy, and the journey would be so much easier if Betty slept. Oh, sod it, I thought, pulling away.

TEN

On Monday, I was delighted to find Dolores loading the dishwasher and humming to herself.

'Have a good weekend?' she asked, pulling an AirPod from one ear.

'Mm, lovely, thanks. Did you enjoy your break?'

'No, I didn't.' She popped her headphone back in and I made myself a coffee.

Luckily, Suzie was more talkative and went straight into a 'deadly dull' garden party she'd gone to. 'Everyone sat on chairs and was dressed in linen, and a woman, also dressed in linen, played the harp.'

'Oh dear,' I said, tempted to make her feel better by relating my Blenheim outing.

'I often wish I'd kept our Camden house,' she said, 'and not this one. London is so much…'

'Livelier?'

'Edgier,' she said. 'I miss edgy.'

I wondered if she'd ever ventured to the Cowley Road. Could I risk blowing my cover and take her there? Maybe not.

'It doesn't help that I can no longer drive,' she added. 'Before the hip ops, I used to nip to London in my gorgeous Mini, stay with friends or in a hotel. It's here in the garage, you know, all taxed and insured.'

'But surely you could drive it again, now you've recovered?'

Suzie shook her head. 'I tried a couple of short trips, but everyone drives so fast now, and what with all those angry people – make that men – honking their horns at me… Terribly rude, I felt.'

'Perhaps you could take a refresher course?'

'Yes!' she said with a clap. 'What a good idea.'

'So, Suzie,' I said, before she asked me to be her instructor, 'what would you like to talk about today?'

'My mother?' she suggested as I pressed the record button. 'Do you know what she used to call me? Often in front of my friends?'

Not wanting to sit through dumplings and boarding school again, I said, 'Why don't you tell me about Pete?'

'Pete?' She frowned at me, head tilted. 'Or Peter?'

'Um…'

'Peter lived in Botley and taught me how to smoke like a pro. I was fourteen, I believe, when we met. No. Yes, almost fifteen. Anyway, Peter had long golden curls and skinny hips and when we first kissed on Port Meadow I thought I might die of bliss.'

'So this wasn't the Pete you married?' Better to get clarification, I thought.

'Gosh, no. What a very different life I'd have had!'

'How long did you and Peter, you know…?'

'Just over a year, then I had to leave the school and help Mummy. One day Daddy drove down to pick me up. It was unexpected and tragic, and I was totally heartbroken. Leaving my friends… my boyfriend. I didn't even know Peter's address, so I couldn't write to him. We'd always met at the same place at the same time, on Saturdays at two thirty, and sort of taken it from there. We'd often arranged an extra clandestine midweek tryst. There were these large bins at the school, you see, next to a six-foot wall. My escape route at night. It was terribly exciting. If something went wrong for one of us, there'd always be the following Saturday at half past two.'

'It sounds very romantic,' I said. 'I can understand why you were so upset.'

'It ate me up that I couldn't contact Peter. I wrote to my two best friends in Oxford, asking them to explain what had happened, if they ever saw him, but neither of them replied. Perhaps my letters were intercepted. Peter's father worked in a bank, that was all I knew. And I had no one else to help me find him. I certainly couldn't tell my parents about Peter.'

'No?'

'No,' she said firmly.

'Have you ever tried to find him since?'

'I did, after my so-called divorce. But, you know, I was never terribly sure of his surname. We just snogged a lot, basically.'

I laughed. 'Ah.'

'It's probably for the best,' Suzie continued. 'He could be morbidly overweight by now. You know, jowls like a bloodhound. I'd have to put him on a diet and take him to my Harley Street chap for a facelift. Get him on Viagra… I think not. As it is, he'll always resemble the young Peter Frampton to me.'

I pulled a 'Who?' face.

'Google him,' suggested Suzie and I got out my phone. Up popped images of a very pretty, very slim boy with hair like an 18th-century gentleman's wig. He was a singer and guitarist.

'Gorgeous,' I told her.

We didn't get to talk more before lunch, as after our stroll around the garden we sat in the kitchen watching Dolores cook and listening to Joey and Lily discussing party drinks.

Suzie seemed to be miles away at times, and I wondered if she was reliving all the snogging. But then, when her eyelids drooped, then sprang open, then drooped again, I realised she was just tired.

'What do you think, Marie?' asked Joey. 'Punch or no punch?'

'Oh, um…' I said, helpfully.

'Absolutely not!' cried Suzie, back with us again. 'Too *Abigail's Party*.'

'You'd need to get a hostess trolley,' I told her.

She laughed. 'And serve cheese and pineapple on sticks.'

While Suzie and I fell about, Joey – who appeared to be blushing – got up from the table and went to his room.

'Oops,' said Dolores.

Suzie sighed. 'He's such a sensitive soul.'

'Tell me about it,' said Dolores.

Lily looked baffled. 'Who's Abigail?'

'Yeah, who is Abigail?' said Dolores.

I got the Mike Leigh play up on my phone and passed it to Lily. 'It's a comedy of manners,' I explained, 'about the pretensions of the newly middle class in the 1970s.'

I expected her to ask what middle class was, but she nodded as she read. 'Ah, I get it now,' she said, looking towards Joey's room.

'I think I might go and rest,' said Suzie.

'Are you OK?' I asked, standing up when she did. 'Would you like me to leave?'

'You take a break, Marie, and I'll see you in the drawing room at, say, one thirty?' She asked Dolores to bring her a tray of food at twelve forty-five – 'With a glass of the usual' – and headed for the stairs.

Lily went to check on Joey, and Dolores and I were left at the table in an awkward silence that I felt compelled to break.

'What did Lily mean about Joey?' I asked. 'That she got it now?'

Dolores shrugged. 'Basically, Joey has an enormous chip on his shoulder. I don't know why. Childhood stuff? Or because he dropped out of Bristol Uni and is working as a carer?'

All went quiet again, so I gave it another go. 'I do like your bracelet.'

'Thanks.'

'You have some very unusual and colourful charms.'

'Yeah.' The bracelet was on top of her sweatshirt sleeve, the cuff of which was folded back a couple of times. Practical for cooking, I guessed. 'It was my granny's but she gave it to me when I was leaving home. I picked up most of the charms on my travels. Some are supposed to bring luck.'

'Can I have a look?' I asked, and she lifted her arm in my direction.

'I never take it off,' she said.

'Never?'

'Well only at airports, where I'm made to. Not even in the bath or shower. At first it was because I didn't want to lose it, or have someone on the yachts steal it. Then I became super superstitious about taking it off.' She looked at it and smiled. 'I adored my grandmother. But the rest of my family can rot in hell.'

'Oh dear,' I said, a bit shocked. 'Do you want to talk about…'

'No. Not really.'

I told her about my own superstitions – like when filling the car, making sure the price came to an even number – then Lily was back, picking up her keys and saying she wouldn't be here for lunch, and Joey wasn't feeling well and just wanted to sleep. Dolores swore and put her headphones in, and I went up to the drawing room to have another hunt for the missing key.

This time I searched amongst the books and photos, and even behind cushions. Suzie's handbag? Where was it? She must have had one, but because Suzie and I hadn't been out together, I'd never actually seen her with a bag of any kind.

After checking the landing, I returned to the desk and opened the lid to rifle through the contents one more time. Crap, crap, rubbish, more tradesmen's business cards… Oh, what was that?

From inside one of the upright compartments, right at the back, I pulled out a thin, ancient-looking, dust-covered book with "Addresses" on the front. A quick flick through its discoloured pages told me it was full of names, addresses and both mobile and landline phone numbers. Some had an email address after them. I went to the C pages and found "Caro (Caroline) Blaine", followed by "(Grandparents)" – Caro's parents had been in Bahrain and uncontactable, presumably. There was nothing in the R pages for Rowena.

I really wanted a good look through, but couldn't do it there. What to do? What to do? My eyes wandered to the ceiling for advice from my dad. 'Take it!' I heard him say, although it sounded more like my voice. 'You can bring it back tomorrow.' Closing the desk lid, I hurried across the room and slid somebody else's property into my laptop bag.

At lunchtime, it was just Dolores and me at the table again, this time eating her roast chicken and ratatouille. Joey was either poorly or sulking in his room.

Dolores talked about Manchester, and the good things to do and see there, then went on to list the amazing places she'd visited, while at sea. It all felt a bit impersonal, but since she loathed her family and didn't know me from Adam, that was understandable.

She asked me about me, and I repeated the ghostwriter story I'd given Suzie, and about the possible move to Wales.

Between courses, Dolores took Suzie her tray and when she returned and had delivered us both a fruit salad with coconut custard, I asked where Joey was from. 'I can't quite pinpoint the accent, not that he has much of one.'

'Leicestershire,' she said, almost whispering. 'His parents are divorced and he's an only child. That's about all I know. Like me, Joey doesn't talk about his family.' She looked up at me and pulled a face. 'So are you coming to this effing party?'

'I think so. You don't sound too keen?'

'Ha, well deduced. I'm definitely at the introvert end of the continuum. Give me a long silent game of Scrabble, any day. We've thrown a few parties here and I always ended up in the attic with a book and my headphones in.' She smiled and her face completely changed. Suddenly, she was quite beautiful. 'I'm not sure anyone's even noticed,' she added.

'Marie!' Suzie called out from the landing. 'Shall we get back to work?'

'I'll be with you in a tick,' I said. 'Just finishing dessert!'

'Bring me a cuppa, could you? Earl Grey. Milk, no sugar.'

'Will do!'

Dolores took her empty bowl to the kitchen, plugged herself in and immediately began humming. I pictured her in the galleys of all those yachts, happily isolating herself in a chef bubble, much as she did in the villa.

* * *

After sinking into the sleep-inducing sofa, I felt more ready for a nap than to record. I stuck a new tape in the machine, and Suzie told me again – in a stream-of-consciousness way – about her childhood home, and about her much-adored nanny, and her mother touring. For a while, I let her run with it, but when I had to pinch myself to stay awake, I butted in.

'I'd love to hear more about Peter,' I said.

'You mean Pete?' she asked.

'No, Peter.'

Suzie's eyes glazed over and she turned and stared through the blinds for a while.

'Your first boyfriend?' I tried again.

She looked my way. 'I think you're getting muddled, Marie. Pete DuBarry was my first proper relationship. He and his group came and played in Dereham. Pete spotted me and got one of the bouncers to invite me backstage. Down to their tiny basement dressing room. It was quite thrilling.'

'So you didn't have a boyfriend while you were at boarding school?'

'I most certainly did not! Do you know what a tight rein they kept us girls on?'

'Oh,' I said. 'OK. My mistake.' I nevertheless took out my phone and flashed the young Peter Frampton at her.

Suzie caught her breath, then leaned back in the sofa and sighed. She closed her eyes for a while, and I resisted closing mine and taking a quick nap.

'It all began,' she said, 'with Miss Davidson, the history teacher. She was waiting for me, arms folded, outside the toilet.'

What was this? I straightened up.

'"Have you just vomited?" she asked me. I nodded and wiped the horrible taste from my lips. I prayed she couldn't smell it. "It's not the first time, is it, Suzie?" I couldn't understand why she was sounding so harsh, so hostile. Normally, she was super nice to me. Telling me how well she thought I'd do at history O-level. Now she frightened me, and I couldn't answer. I was terribly embarrassed, too. Had she been listening to me retching? My face burning up, I ran to the basins and washed my mouth out. Miss Davidson then marched me to the sick room near my dorm and handed me over to Matron.'

'Was it a bug?' I asked.

Suzie went quiet for a bit, frowning at whatever was in her head. 'I listened to them whispering outside but didn't catch any of it. And then Matron came in. She shut the door and sat on a chair beside the camp bed I was lying on. And then she asked me some very personal questions.'

'Oh?'

'And then Daddy came for me.' Suzie stared into her lap, for so long that I considered pressing pause. Then she turned to me with a pained expression.

'It was being hidden away that was the very worst part,' she said. 'Basically locked up. On no account was anyone to see me. Luckily, for Mummy, I had no friends locally. My old primary school pals had moved on to different secondary schools and different friends. I'd watch my mother getting ready to leave the house, putting the padding on over her underwear, followed by a voluminous maternity dress.' Suzie smiled. 'You couldn't do crop top and a big bare belly back then!'

I chuckled nervously in the silence.

'No,' she said after a pause. 'You had to hide your bump as best you could, luckily for Mummy. As I grew bigger, so did she.' Suzie looked at me and smiled. 'As much as Mummy hated the situation, she loved the acting experience it afforded her. So much so that she'd often stay in character when she got home. The hand in the arch of her back, the way she lowered herself into an armchair.'

Suzie's expression changed. 'An ancient, retired GP would pay me visits privately, and put his hands and fingers where I felt sure they didn't need to go. I was only fifteen at that point, and knew nothing, so I gritted my teeth and bore it. After a few months an equally ancient, retired midwife came instead. She wasn't all that nice but at least she didn't feel me up. When I reached my due date, Mummy took me to a house in Northampton for a few days. She fed me castor oil to get the labour started, and it worked.' Suzie finished her drink and stared into the empty glass. 'The same midwife arrived there and stayed three days. I'd imagine it cost Mummy a fortune in private medical bills, but it kept things… well, me, under the radar.

Would she say any more, I wondered, before denying it all tomorrow?

'I went through sheer bloody hell, but the result was a beautiful little boy.' Suzie smiled to herself. 'Mummy, rather uncharacteristically, told me she was terribly proud of me. So much so that she let me name the baby after my favourite singer.'

In the silence that followed, while my heart thumped loudly in my ears, I tried not to speak and break the spell.

'Dylan,' she said, as I knew she would.

ELEVEN

As I was pouring milk onto the kids' granola and muesli mix, a text arrived on the mobile Dylan had given me.

> *Sorry Marie, but Suzie is having blood taken today, a hospital appointment tomorrow, and her hair done Thursday. Then we'll all be preparing for the party. She sends her apologies and looks forward to seeing you on Saturday, 7 p.m. onwards. Remember to bring people! Joey*

The message was worrying. Why was she going to the hospital, and actually was she really? A bigger concern was the address book I'd taken photos of and which I'd planned to return that day. I took it out of the laptop bag and tapped it against my hand while I thought. Or tried to. Apparently, I'd poured too much milk on the kids' cereal whilst reading Joey's text. Betty was tipping it back in the milk carton and getting it all over the island and her clothes.

'Muuuum,' yelled Maeve from the mirror. 'You'll have to change her!'

I girded my loins and led a wet and distressed Betty – 'I want my granola!' – upstairs, where I promised her the much-preferred, hidden-in-my-room Coco Pops, if she calmed the hell down.

'We'll just have to wait for Mummy to leave,' I added. Daddy, who was to pick them up at eight twenty, was more phlegmatic about these things.

After they'd all gone and I was dealing with the morning chaos, which would later be replaced by the evening chaos, I came across Suzie's address book. It was spreadeagled under a tea towel, soaking up a puddle of brown Coco-Pops milk. I swore and frantically tried dabbing it dry, but a chunk of the pages were melded together by liquid and would have torn if I'd tried peeling them apart. I paced and fretted. Would anyone notice it was missing? Unlikely. After all, it had been tucked away and was very dusty when I'd found it. But then again…

I decided to lie on the sofa to calm down and empty my head of all thoughts. To be in the now and not catastrophise. 'An old address book,' I told myself. 'That's all it is.'

I repeated my mantra for a while, but then that unexpected text from Joey careered into my imaginary walk beside a babbling brook. Perhaps I'd been rumbled, or was at least under suspicion. Had Suzie decided she'd given away too much? Was what she'd told me even true?

When I'd done a video call with Mike and Emily last night, Mike had been sceptical. 'She's what we call an unreliable narrator in English Lit,' he'd said.

The three of us had then made the decision to keep it to ourselves, at least for now, and I'd tucked away the cassette in a locked cash box in my wardrobe.

What I needed was a distraction. I picked up my phone and tapped on a number.

'Hi,' I said.

'Hey,' Greg said back. 'How are you?'

'Good. How free are you?'

'For you, completely. Just give me half an hour to finish a chapter?' Greg had recently reduced his teaching hours in order to write a psychology textbook, making daytime outings and get-togethers more doable.

'See you then,' I said, getting the usual Greg-related butterflies.

After quickly letting Dylan know about the message from Joey, I showered and spent twenty minutes choosing something to wear and another ten choosing something else. I sprayed stuff on my hair to make it shine, and dabbed stuff on my face to make it not shine, then, just in case, shoved overnight things in a rucksack.

TWELVE

After a chilled few days at Greg's house, then mine, and in the office, Saturday evening arrived. Emily turned up at my house with Flo and a worried expression. 'Ben couldn't get away to look after her,' she told Mike and me. 'Some big investigation. And Mum and Dad are on a city break. Sorry, Edie. I know I don't *have* to come along to this party… only I really, really want to.'

'No problem,' I said. 'Perhaps we could all go in your car, then you'll be able to leave the party when you and Flo have had enough. We'll taxi back.'

'Ah thanks, Edie.'

Astrid then rolled up wearing her middle-aisle dress. 'Not a word,' she told me, eyes narrowed. I crossed my heart and hoped to die.

Ten minutes later we were strapped into Emily's Golf and on our way to the villa – Mike in the front, and Astrid and me in the back next to Flo in her car seat. Nursery rhymes came out of the speakers and, apart from Astrid, we were all singing along. 'And when they were up, they were up…'

When we arrived the front drive was full, so Emily parked on the road. Flo was transferred to her pushchair and three bottles of wine stuck out of the tray beneath her. We all laughed and Emily took a photo.

When we walked through the villa's open door, I felt even more nervous than I had on my first visit. Perhaps it was the slightly too short LBD I was wearing, which was old and not as nice as Astrid's. It didn't help my nerves, either, when Emily took three steps into the hall and stopped dead, her face draining of colour. What with 'Napgate' it occurred to me she might be pregnant and about to faint.

When Suzie practically flew across the hall at us and said, 'Hurrah! Now who's this little darling?' Emily recovered and said, 'Florence, but we call her Flo.'

'No, no, no,' cried Suzie. 'Don't let them call you that. You're a beautiful Florence, aren't you, sweetie. My very favourite city.'

I introduced Suzie, and then my friends. We'd decided that, to avoid confusion, everyone would go by their own names. Apart from me, of course.

Over Suzie's shoulder I saw Dylan approaching with a vexed expression. Damn. Should I have run my guest list past him? We hadn't spoken for the past four days and only a small part of me expected him to be here.

Suzie linked arms with him. 'Everyone, this is my brother, Dylan.'

'Nice to meet you,' I said. 'I'm Marie.'

'Ah, you're helping my sister with her sizzling autobiography?' His mouth smiled, his eyes didn't.

'That's the plan,' I said, then introduced the others.

Emily took Flo out of her buggy and Mike collapsed it and laid it beside the French thing. 'Gorgeous credenza,' he told Suzie, who'd managed to steal Flo from Emily.

'It is,' I agreed. OK, not French.

Suzie stopped blowing raspberries at Flo. 'Pete picked it up for a song in the eighties,' she said. 'He's here somewhere. Probably telling rock-star whoppers in the garden.'

'Undoubtedly,' said Dylan. He was in blue jeans and a fleece, and had a can in his hand. If it hadn't been for the unlit cigar in his other hand, you might not have taken him for a top restaurateur. 'My favourite Belgian white beer,' he said, raising the can. 'Unfiltered and with a hint of coriander, orange zest and pink peppercorns.' He drank some and pulled an appreciative face. 'Brought my own stash,' he added before wandering off.

'Shall we go and find Petey-Weety?' Suzie asked a mesmerised Flo.

When Joey came out of his room, locking the door with a key, he turned and looked surprised to see us all.

'Hey! Welcome, welcome!' he said, and I did the introductions one more time and we all wished him a happy birthday.

After he'd pointed out a group of five guys as his fellow football players, we followed him to what he called, 'Dolores and Lily's buffet extraordinaire.'

I felt bad about not bringing a present. I hadn't been able to think of anything, so preoccupied had I been with finding a party outfit. Unsuccessfully, obviously. And besides, what do you give someone who has the pick of all Suzie's things?

'It's this way for the booze, Edie!' shouted Astrid, heading towards the long kitchen counter heaving with bottles. 'Oops! I mean, Marie, ha ha!'

I pretended not to know her and hovered around the impressive offerings, not feeling hungry enough for it yet. While I watched Astrid pour a glass of red, I decided that, if confronted about my name, I could always say I used Marie professionally, for the sake of discretion.

Once Astrid was safely out in the garden, I poured myself a large glass of white, drank some and topped it up again, then went and sat in an armchair beside the albums and record player. It was a good spot to people watch, and even gave me a view of the patio. On it stood Pete DuBarry, all Brian May hair and skinny jeans, puffing on a roll-up. With a deep and gravelly voice that carried, he was entertaining a group of what looked like more footballers, waving his arms around and chortling.

When Suzie approached him, carrying Flo, Pete stopped performing and slipped an arm around them both. Flicking his cigarette butt into a bush, he then reached for Flo, but she screamed so loudly that Emily dropped her plate of food on a chair and hurried to the garden. Before she got there, Flo was squeezing Suzie's nose and chuckling, and Emily left them to it.

I watched Joey bouncing around the room, getting kissed on the cheeks, having group selfies taken, and occasionally being handed a present. More people arrived and milled. Dolores waved at me from where she stood alone on the periphery, leaning against the newel post at the bottom of the stairs. She was in her standard outfit of black polo-style top and loose black trousers. She looked a bit excluded, and I was on the verge of getting up to go and talk to her when Lily approached me, holding a real camera and asking if she could take my photo. I caught Dylan giving me a don't-you-dare stare.

'Actually, would you mind if we didn't?' I laughed, and added, 'Not looking my best this evening.'

'No prob,' said Lily, 'although you look great to me!'

I thanked her and she wandered off, and I realised, what with the number of selfies being taken, that I could have already been tagged all over social media.

Food, I thought again, but got distracted by Dolores leading Emily and Flo to her bedroom, probably for a nappy change. I considered going and helping but didn't want anyone stealing my comfy chair.

The truth was, I couldn't face getting into bullshit conversations about who I was and how I knew Joey, etc. Aware, though, that I couldn't just sit in an armchair all evening, I prayed for some loud music to go on, and after another ten minutes of Dylan blanking me, and Mike doing a great job of mingling, my wish came true and live music wafted in from the garden.

'Come on, Marie!' said Joey, beside me and holding out his hand. 'We know you love a waltz!'

'Oh, blimey,' I said. 'OK.'

Once on my feet, he gave me an unexpected hug, then leaned back and beamed at me. 'I'm so pleased you came, you know. You're beginning to feel like one of the family.'

'Aah,' I said, 'it's nice of you to say that.' I wondered how sincere he was being, since I'd hardly been coming there for months. Or even weeks. He didn't seem drunk, but perhaps he'd partaken of something else. Or he was just a nice guy – one who liked taking care of Suzie and making the house run smoothly and happily. 'I do enjoy hanging out here,' I added. 'And Lily seems very nice.'

'Yeah, she's amazing. I'm pretty sure she's the one. Finally!'

'Wow.'

'Between you and me, I was thinking of spontaneously proposing tonight. Only, you know, I think you're supposed to have a ring?' He laughed. 'But listen, we should plan an evening out somewhere soon. The four of us, or five with Lily. And you could bring your guy. Mike, is it?'

'Oh, we're–'

'What's your favourite kind of food?'

I had a think. 'Thai?'

'Correct answer! I'll book us a table in Jericho. Monday OK?'

'I think so,' I said, as I finished my drink and put the glass on the big table. 'Can I let you know tomorrow?'

'Of course.'

I looked at the food and suddenly felt hungry. When had I last eaten?

'To the dance floor!' said Joey, ushering me outside. 'I love Random Angels.'

The band was playing acoustically at the bottom of the garden. I recognised it as a Floors song, and Pete was making a valiant effort with the vocals. Astrid was shaking her Lidl dress directly in front of the best-looking Random Angel, and Joey, beside me, began flicking one hand at the sky while shaking his head from side to side. Lily took photos as the footballers and a few older people – who could have been Joey's relatives or Suzie's neighbours – joined in. I rather boringly wondered how the poor lawn would feel tomorrow.

I danced for a while, then two songs later remembered Emily and Flo and went in search of them. I was going to offer to keep an eye on Flo, if Emily wanted to watch the band, have a dance, and maybe get a selfie with Pete. Ben was a fan of The Floors, apparently, and played their songs with his own band.

Emily wasn't in the kitchen-diner area, so I tapped on Dolores's door and called out, 'Emily?'

No answer. When I went to open the door, I found it locked. Like Joey, Dolores was sensibly keeping the guests out. I turned around and, not for the first time, was bothered by the keys dangling from brass hooks on a "Skegness is so Bracing" rack. They were hung way too close to the breakable original glass panel in the front door. 'The burglar's favourite gift,' my dad used to say.

Spotting that the pushchair had gone from the hall, I popped out to the street to check if they'd left. But no, the Golf was still there and they weren't in it. Emily was nowhere to be seen on the ground floor, or in the garden, and I had a vision of them up on the top floor in the cosy reading room. Flo asleep on the futon. I began making my way there, stopping en route to use the first-floor loo. The room had three tiled walls, a toilet, a basin and a shower. I wondered if this was for Suzie's staff to use, since there were two large washbags on a low shelf, and two sets of towels, one black, one colourful.

While in there, I heard voices coming from the drawing room. Judging by how loud they were, I guessed the dividing wall was made of a single sheet of plasterboard. This shower room must have been created out of the original middle bedroom that had been opened up to the master, making Suzie's L-shaped drawing room.

Even if made of plasterboard, I thought, the conversation between Suzie and Emily was particularly clear. Why, I wondered, was there a small mirror hanging next to the very large mirror above the basin? What, or who, was it there for? Or was it hiding a stain? Lifting it gently off its hook, I saw a series of holes had been made in the plasterboard behind it. They were small enough to make you think someone had taken several goes at trying to hang the mirror, but big enough to let anything said in the drawing room filter through. I peered into one hole, but couldn't see anything. A plant, perhaps.

'Aww,' I heard Emily say, now even louder. 'Must have been a nightmare?'

'Oh, it was,' said Suzie.

'Well it's been lovely chatting,' said Emily, 'but I'd better get this little one home.'

'And I must organise cake and singing. Thanks for the astrological reading, Emily.'

'You're welcome.'

I quickly rehung the mirror, opened the door and was on the landing when Suzie came out, wheeling the pushchair with a sleeping, horizontal Flo in it.

'Ah, there you are!' I said to Emily. 'I came to look for you. See if you wanted to have a dance while I look after Flo.'

'Yeah, all right,' she said. 'Thanks. Suzie was watching Flo but cos of the noise downstairs, she kept *almost* falling asleep, then waking up. So Suzie carried her upstairs. In the pushchair, can you believe?'

'Wow,' I said. 'Impressive.'

'Stronger than I look,' said Suzie. 'Have you been shown my garden gym?'

'No?'

'The black building behind the acacia. It was Dolores's idea.'

'I'd love to see it,' I lied.

'Flo's dead to the world now,' said Emily. 'You could even put her on stage next to Pete and she wouldn't wake up. Suzie, aren't you worried the neighbours will complain and the police might turn up?'

Suzie snorted. 'I hear a cacophony of Radio Fours blasting out at full volume all day, every day. Believe me, the entire elderly street is deaf. Oh, am I allowed to say that?'

'Only to us, maybe?' said Emily. 'Come on then, let's carry this–'

'It's OK,' said Suzie, lifting up the pushchair and sleeping child. 'I can manage. Weight-bearing exercise. All good.'

My heart was in my mouth until a noticeably shaking Suzie got to the bottom, where she put the buggy down and rushed off, and Emily went strange again; pale-faced and staring into space.

'Em?' I said. 'Are you all right?'

'Yeah, yeah. Only I think I will get this little one home and into her own bed.'

'If you're sure? You haven't seen the band play, or met Pete?'

'I'm good,' she said. 'And Ben's the big Floors fan, not me. Maybe you could get Pete's signature for him, or like a photo?'

'OK, I'll try.' While I walked with her to the car, I asked what she and Suzie had been talking about.

'Childbirth,' she said quietly. 'And how effing awful it is. She was telling me what her mum went through when she had Dylan, only we're not sure it was her mum, are we?'

'No, we're not. Best to keep that under our hats.'

'Hundred per cent.'

While Emily strapped Flo in, I loaded the buggy into the boot. We had a quick hug goodbye and arranged to have a midday meeting on Monday. As I started to walk away, she lowered her window and glanced at the villa then looked back at me.

'I dunno, Edie,' she said, 'but maybe you should...'

'What?'

'Oh nothing. Nothing at all.' She slowly pulled away. 'See you Monday!'

* * *

Everyone had been asked to gather in the garden and guests were slowly drifting out of the kitchen. While the band began putting their instruments away, some quieter hip-hop track had replaced them and a few people carried on dancing. Astrid, of course, was one of them. And so were Mike and a couple of footballers.

Meanwhile, Dolores and Lily carried a small table to the middle of the garden, then Lily went and fetched a huge brown football cake with, presumably, thirty-five candles on it.

Suzie followed with a stack of small plates and a large knife. 'Do we have any chilled champagne left?'

'Can I do anything?' I asked.

'I think we're fine,' said Lily. 'But thanks. I'll just take some cake shots for Insta.'

'I'm told you're the biographer?' said a gruff voice behind me.

I spun around to find Pete beaming at me. I wondered if he and Suzie used the same cosmetic dentist.

'Cos I could tell you a wild tale or two about our hoity-toity Suze.'

'Yes, I am,' I said. 'Marie. Nice to meet you.' For some reason, I scanned the garden for Dylan. No sign of him. I wondered if he and Pete had conversed at all. 'Suzie's great,' I added. 'I really like her.'

'And I adore you too,' said Suzie, sidling up to me and squeezing my shoulder. 'Marie was an actress, did she tell you? Now where the hell is the birthday boy? I texted him to come to the garden.'

'I'll go and get him,' said Dolores.

'And I'll fetch the champers,' said Suzie.

'An actress, eh?' asked Pete, when she'd gone.

'Actually, no. But I've interviewed a fair few.'

'And I've *had* a fair few,' he said with a smirk. He went on to give me a long and explicit account of a drugs-and-sex escapade he'd had with one of our veteran national treasures. 'She was an absolute cracker back then,' he said, winding it up. 'Now she's playing Miss Havisham. Pretty tragic what happens to beautiful women, don't you think?'

I looked into the rheumy eyes of his crumpled, age-spotted, bag-of-walnuts face, stuck for a response. 'Listen, Pete,' I said. 'You couldn't do me a huge favour, could you?'

'Not if it involves money, I couldn't. Got three ex-wives taking every penny and forcing me to tour with a bunch of kids who don't know their King Crimson from their Hawkwind.'

'Sounds ghastly. No, it's not money, don't worry.' I asked if I could take a short video of him saying 'Hi' to Emily. 'She wanted to meet you because her husband's a huge Floors fan. His own band even plays your songs. Only she had to bring her little girl, Flo, along this evening, and now she's had to leave, and–'

'Little Florence? Yeah, I met her. Suzie was quite smitten. Shame she didn't want kids of her own. I begged her, you know, but she was adamant.'

'Really?' This differed from Dylan's version – that they hadn't been able to conceive.

'If you ask me,' said Pete, 'I reckon we'd still be together if we'd had a couple of sprogs.'

I gave him a sceptical look.

'Yeah, right, who am I kidding,' he said, laughing. 'I was a right randy bastard back then.' He pointed at my phone. 'OK, let's do this, shall we? What's her husband the musician's name?'

'Ben. He's actually a police officer.' I laughed at Pete's look of disgust, then I put my phone on video and said, 'Three, two, one… Go.'

'Hi there, Emma, Ben and Florence…'

I stopped filming and said, 'Sorry, Pete. It's Emily, Ben and Flo.'

'Got it.'

'Three, two, one… Go.'

'Hi there, Emily, Bill… Shit, I was thinking of the Old Bill.'

I laughed and started filming again, when a terrifying scream came from above. I looked up and watched with horror as a body tumbled through the darkness towards us, somewhere to my left.

There was a loud thump, and at the same time a yellow shoe with white laces bounced off the cake table and landed, the right way up, on the grass.

THIRTEEN

There was a brief lull when only hip hop could be heard, before the screams and shouting and panic kicked off. Despite feeling shocked, horrified and mildly nauseous, something told me to keep my phone, still on video, running.

I filmed Astrid clinging to a handsome black footballer, and Mike heading my way. And Pete saying, 'Stone the fucking crows.'

Then when Mike reached me, I said, 'Go and check the side gate, can you? Make sure it's locked. And block that route off, if that's possible. And then call 999. Oh, and go and lock the front door, yeah? The key… "Skegness is so Bracing"… can't miss it.'

Mike looked suitably overloaded and confused, but immediately strode off, while I continued to film in a panoramic way, left to right. I walked to the kitchen and filmed in there. 'You're shaking,' said a woman I didn't know. She laughed and I realised news of what had happened hadn't yet spread that far. I went through to the dining area and did a slow pirouette, then there was Mike again, at the far end of the hall, guarding the front door and staring at his phone.

I walked up the stairs, phone pointing towards the top.

'What's all the hubbub about?' asked Suzie, on her way down. 'Has something happened?'

'Mike!' I called back to him, and I pointed at Suzie.

'Coming!' he said, taking the stairs two at a time. He embraced Suzie, turning her around and leading her back up.

'Tell me!' she shouted, as she disappeared into the drawing room.

The door to the loo opened when I tried it, but I still double-checked no one was in there. With the landing empty, I was tempted to take the stairs to the top floor, but at the bottom I held back, turned around and entered the drawing room, phone aloft. There I found Dylan holding his sister's hand on the green sofa.

Mike hovered nearby. 'I'll go and watch the door again,' he said. 'The police and ambulance should be here soon.'

'The police?' cried Dylan, leaping up and going to the window. 'What the hell for? What's happened? I'm a well-known restaurateur you know. I can't get caught up in… will you *please* stop filming me, Edie!'

'Who's Edie?' asked Suzie, while Mike reversed out of the room.

I lowered my phone but didn't switch it off, then began quietly explaining to them that there'd been an accident, but I wasn't quite sure what had happened, or who was involved.

Leaving them to it, and with my phone still filming, I once again, stopped short of going up to the attic and contaminating the potential scene of an accident or crime. My guess was that an off-his-head footballer had been pratting around on that dangerous little balcony and toppled off.

But maybe… Something told me to go up there. After looking over both shoulders, I videoed my way up the stairs – heart thumping – past the dressing room-cum-library and into the back attic room.

I hadn't known what to expect, but what I found was a lot of mess and no people. The doors were open and I bravely or stupidly – someone could be out there ready to pounce – approached the balcony. There in the semi-darkness were various bits and pieces, bottles and cans and half-plates of food, all strewn across the floor, along with the chair cushions. Having filmed all that, I went back in, did a 360 of the lit-up room and its contents, then switched off the camera and ran all the way down to the safety of Mike.

At the sound of a siren, he unlocked the door to reveal two paramedics running towards us.

'That was quick,' I said, then remembered how near we were to the hospital.

'Can you wait here and let the police in?' Mike asked me.

While he took the paramedics through the house, I relocked the door and sat on top of the key on the lilac chair. I'd stopped shaking and now just felt numb and light-headed.

I thought of my late dad, and how some of the things he'd related when I was little – in the car, on walks, on the beach – had come back to me in an emergency. 'We had to detain them in the theatre until we'd interviewed all ninety-three. Everyone's a suspect until they're not. Luckily for us, the wedding photographer had carried on snapping the guests, so we knew where they'd been shortly after the attack.'

A wave of noise built up. It was coming from the kitchen. One woman shrieked loudly. And then again. God, all that wonderful food in there and I was stuck guarding the door. So hungry… why hadn't I eaten something earlier? People were shouting, someone screamed, someone wailed.

'Oh, there you are, Edie,' said Astrid. 'I've called for a cab. Want to share with James and me?'

I guessed James was the handsome footballer. 'We can't go,' I said. 'Not yet.'

'Of course we can.' She tried the front door and swore. 'Come on, Edie. Give me the key. Argh, where *is* James? Or is it Jamie? The taxi won't wait long.'

'The police are on their way,' I told her. 'They may need to talk to everyone.'

Astrid disappeared, but more guests filled the hall – mostly the footballers – and one tried the door. I told them it was locked, and why, and after attempting to get into Joey and Dolores's rooms to escape through a window, they drifted back to the noisy mêlée.

'What a bore,' said Astrid, back again. 'That Dolores woman tops herself and I have to spend hours hanging around in this *Old Curiosity Shop* meets *Rocky Horror*…'

What was she saying? Dolores? *Our* Dolores? Dead?

'Jamie!' said Astrid, when her man arrived.

'Jake,' he corrected her.

'Listen, hon, we're going to have to jump a back fence or two, since the side gate won't open. See you, Edie. Edie? Shit, are you all right? Edie!'

I felt my face being slapped, but it didn't hurt, and then I was sliding off the chair with no arms.

'Edie!' yelled Astrid. 'Christ, she's passing out. Why's everyone keeling over or falling off buildings? Have we all been poisoned? Jake, go and get Mike. What? Yes, the big guy. Yes, gay. Quick!'

As I was being propped up by Astrid, Joey came out of his room, pulling headphones from his ears. 'Is it cake time?' he asked.

FOURTEEN

On Sunday the three of us met in the office at midday. I went first.

'OK, so, as I told the police last night… if three in the morning counts as last night?'

'I think it might,' said Mike. He looked as exhausted as I felt.

I yawned, apologised and continued. 'Although I'd heard Dolores crying in her room, I hadn't got to know her well enough to say she might have been suicidal.'

'Also,' said Mike, 'I'm no expert, but I'm pretty sure people who jump don't cry out.'

'I think I've heard that,' I said. 'But why would anyone want to push her?'

Emily sighed. 'She seemed really nice. And kind. Offered me her room to change Flo. She even took her pooey nappy away. She wasn't exactly talkative, but, yeah, kind.'

'I didn't get to speak to her,' said Mike.

Emily tapped her chin with her phone. 'There *was* something a bit odd,' she said, frowning. 'You know how tidy Dolores's room is?'

I shook my head. 'Never been in it.'

'Like absolutely nothing was out of place, and the bed was all neatly made. I was sitting on it for a while, cuddling Flo and trying to get her off to sleep. She likes *Twinkle, Twinkle* at bedtime, only it wasn't working. So we were there for a while, and I tried *Baa, Baa Black Sheep*, and *Mary Had a Little…*'

'Mike!' I said, clapping to wake him.

'Sorry,' he said, shifting himself upright. 'Sorry. Carry on, Em.'

'OK… well, then I noticed a board and some tiles on the floor, like they'd fallen off this, like, table and hadn't been put back? Anyway, I went and picked it up, and it turned out to be a Scrabble board.'

'Dolores is a Scrabblehead,' I said. 'Was. She even did tournaments.'

'Surely that would be a sign of depression?' asked Mike.

'Please don't,' I told him.

'So…' Emily continued, 'I went and picked it up, along with the eight tiles. And anyway I sort of played around with the tiles, and then I realised…'

'Yes?' I asked.

'OK, look. I'll tell you guys the letters and you see what you make, yeah?'

She gave us each a pen and a piece of paper and reeled off the letters. I wrote mine down in a straight line, while Mike, I noticed, formed a circle.

'Fuck you y?' he asked.

'Wow, you're quick,' said Emily.

'Do we think she was going to make it Joey?' I asked.

'Or Lily?' asked Mike. He folded his arms and scowled. 'What speculatory route exactly are we heading down here? That Dolores put those words on the board and either Joey or Lily took offence and pushed her off a terrace? An extreme response, wouldn't you say?'

'But Joey was in his room,' said Emily.

I nodded. 'And Lily was in the garden.'

'When did either of you last see Dolores?' asked Emily.

Mike shrugged. 'I wasn't even introduced to her, so…'

'In the garden,' I said, 'after the table and cake were set up, Suzie couldn't get a response from Joey, so Dolores said she'd look for him. Obviously, that had involved going to the balcony. I'm sure the police will work out roughly where everyone was.'

'Thanks to you recording the scene,' said Emily.

The detective, who'd arrived half an hour after the uniformed officers, had asked me to forward my video to him. 'And Lily was taking photos throughout,' I told Emily. 'Others had been filming too, what with Pete and the band playing.'

'I reckon you'll get the Best Director Oscar, though,' said Emily, laughing. 'Sorry, shouldn't be making jokes.'

'Too right,' said Mike. 'Not if I can't.'

'We could all watch my video together,' I suggested. 'And maybe spot something?'

'How about when we're not so knackered?' suggested Mike. He yawned and rubbed at his bristly cheeks. 'Dylan's a strange guy, isn't he?'

I pulled a face. 'Strange in what way?'

'Guarded. Tense. We mostly talked about property prices, and I got the impression that was deliberate. Safe territory. He watched you like a hawk, Edie. At least all the time I was with him.'

'Really? I didn't notice. I did think he was pissed off with me for turning up with my co-workers. Worried one of us might spill the beans.'

'And what *about* all this cloak-and-dagger stuff?' asked Mike. 'What was that for?'

I tried to think about what Mike had just said, but thinking wasn't coming easily. As well as being upset and in shock, I was stupendously sleep-deprived, having been woken at six – an hour after finally dropping off – by Betty and her full-volume tablet. She'd shown me her new game while I'd groped around the edges of the device for the volume control. Like every game the kids had ever shown me, it involved running and crashing into something, then getting up and running and crashing into something else. I'd suspected Betty of just playing at playing, but Jack swore babies were born with gaming skills these days.

'Good point,' I told Mike. 'Was all the subterfuge necessary?'

'Look,' he said, 'are we really going to get anywhere with this now? And do we need to?'

Emily shook her head. 'I only came to check you were both all right.'

'I'm surprisingly all right,' said Mike. 'Considering I saw the body.' He stood up and stretched his arms. 'I'm heading back to bed. I suggest we meet again tomorrow, during Em's lunch break?'

I agreed. 'By then, the police might know more.'

'Shame it's in the wrong area for Ben,' said Emily. 'But I'm sure he'll be able to find out stuff for us.'

'That might be useful,' I said, 'but who knows? I'm guessing Dylan won't want my services any longer, but I'll update you both if I hear anything.'

When Mike had gone I bit the bullet. 'I haven't told you about Dolores's shoes, Em.'

'Oh yeah? What about…' She stopped and stared at me. 'Don't tell me they were yellow?'

'They were.'

'Shit, I didn't notice.'

'I didn't, either. Not until one fell in front of me in the garden. She was wearing those long baggy black trousers that must have covered her shoes.'

Emily suddenly looked pale and pained, so I went and got her some water and she took a few sips.

'If I'd noticed,' she whispered, 'maybe she'd still be alive. I could have got her to change her shoes. You know, like spilt something on them?'

'Now you're being silly.'

'Thing is, I had this bad feeling? Like when I walked in, and other times. I so wanted to tell you to leave, you know.'

Not pregnant then, just psychic.

'Don't tell Ben,' she added and I promised I wouldn't.

I gave her a hug, then we locked up the office and headed to our respective homes. Two bouncing children would be a welcome distraction, I thought, but when I got to the house, peace reigned. Alfie and Betty were with Jack, and Maeve had her laptop, books and notes spread out on our kitchen island. Her black curly hair was held back with a pretty turban-style floral headband.

'Is that new?' I asked, pointing at it.

'It is, yeah. A girl on my course makes them. I could get you one, if you like. Here, try it on.'

Maeve pulled the little scarf off and handed it to me. 'How are you?' she asked.

'Awful.' I put on the headband and went over to the mirror. 'But sleep might help.'

'I made a spicy rice thing for lunch. Fancy some?'

'Just a little. Thanks.' I had to remember to eat. My almost passing out at Suzie's was probably down to lack of food. And a shocking death, of course.

'I'll make you a small bowl. Glass of wine? Brandy for shock?'

I shook my head. Following last night's incident and my reaction, I'd helped myself to food and wine. And once the police had left, more wine.

'Oh, Lord,' I said on seeing myself in the mirror. 'Maeve, how come you look like an exotic temptress from a fifties movie in it, and I look like a cleaner topping up her pension?'

'Let's see?' she said, then rolled around on her stool, giggling. 'Sorry, but you shouldn't have put that in my head.'

I handed it back, now despondent as well as knackered, and went and poured two glasses of water for us.

When we sat opposite each other and dug in, Maeve looked at me tentatively. 'Do you want to tell me more about it?' she asked.

I'd given her a short summary when she'd woken up at nine forty-five and I'd handed over the kids. Maeve had always slept well – a blessing when she'd been a baby, but a tad irritating now. It had certainly irritated Jack.

'I still can't take it in,' I said.

'I bet. Did you actually see her falling?'

'I did. Initially, I thought it was a man. There were lots of young footballers there, you see.'

'And you didn't invite me! Actually, thank God you didn't.'

'It was dark and Dolores was wearing black. Black shirt, black trousers. She made this terrifying noise as she fell, which could have come from a man or a woman. I was worried that he or she would land on someone, but apparently Dolores hit the flat roof of Suzie's gym.'

'Jesus, Mum. That's so tragic. Did you like her? Dolores? How old was she?'

'Mid-thirties, I think. And, yes, as far as I got to know her, she seemed nice. Quite reserved. A fabulous cook. Professional chef, you know?'

'Wow.'

'She and I were forced to waltz together on my first day. By Suzie. That was funny.' I could feel myself tearing up. 'The last time we chatted, she told me she hated parties.'

Maeve got off her stool and came and gave me a hug and a piece of kitchen roll. 'Are you sure you wouldn't rather teach eight-year-olds again?'

'Actually, no,' I said, sniffing and dabbing my eyes. 'Right now, I'm really not sure.'

'Listen, I've still got some of those knock-out tablets, left over from when I was post-natal and couldn't sl–'

'Yes please.'

FIFTEEN

I woke up utterly refreshed – God those things were good – and reached for my phone. The story had hit the local news but, as far as I could see, not the nationals. The *Oxford Mail* report was one short paragraph saying a woman had suffered a fatal fall from a balcony in the Summertown area on Saturday evening, and that an investigation was being carried out. No name was given, thank goodness. I quickly shut down the article and got up, so as not to relive it.

After a rushed family breakfast, post-weekend housework, and a shower, I walked around the corner to my office just before eleven, hovering over calling Dylan but deciding to wait until I'd met with Mike and Emily at midday.

With time to spare, I popped out to the local stationers and bought a large piece of white card, then back at my desk I rewatched my video of the party, beginning with

Pete getting the names wrong, and ending with the balcony.

The footage – with Dolores's howl and the screams that followed – disturbed me more than it had when I'd last watched it, early Sunday morning when I'd still felt numb. This time, my stomach knotted up and my heart both raced and ached, and before I knew it I was back in the Blenheim maze terrified that I'd lost Alfie. Then I was on the London Eye with a psychopath, listening to an unsettling message from Emily, then back in that maze, calling and calling for my grandson.

I got up and paced around, taking deep breaths and hoping the others wouldn't arrive early and catch me being so affected. So weak. Everything's fine, I told myself.

* * *

It turned out Mike was something of an artist and the plans of Suzie's house that he'd drawn with a Sharpie, and a little guidance from me, were spot on. The ground-floor footprint was larger due to two extensions, while the first- and second-floor footprints were the same, even though the attic felt much smaller.

'It's the low sloping walls,' he explained. 'Like that famous optical illusion of two lines?'

He and Emily were nailing the plans to the wall that clients never looked at, below the clock they didn't see me checking.

'Ooh, I love Cluedo,' Emily said, as step by step we went through my video.

We let Mike draw the figures, while Emily and I instructed him. First he drew himself and Astrid by the stage, along with Jake the footballer and someone called Dean, who Mike had been dancing with.

'Pete was beside me,' I told him.

'Here?' he asked. 'Near the cake table?'

'Yes. And Lily was there too, waiting for Joey and looking mildly pissed off.'

'And Joey was here, in his room?' Mike asked.

'Yep.'

We restarted the video and next Mike drew Suzie and Dylan in the drawing room upstairs. Since Mike had mingled more than we had, he watched the footage from the beginning and shook his head.

'The four people I chatted to, apart from Dylan and Joey, were all in the garden.'

Cluedo over, but not yet solved, we all stood in front of the floor plans, arms folded.

'OK,' said Mike. 'Assuming Joey was in his room and oblivious, who could have been on the balcony with Dolores, if indeed anyone was?'

'Suzie,' I suggested, and Mike put a red circle next to her.

'And Dylan,' said Emily. 'I reckon Joey's a suspect too. He could've quickly run down the two lots of stairs and into his room without anyone noticing.'

'At a stretch,' I said. 'He did sound pretty convincing, coming out of his room and asking about cake. But then I had just blacked out.'

Emily put an arm around me and said, 'Aww.'

'So who are we plumping for?' asked Mike, putting the tops back on his pens. 'Colonel Mustard?'

'Unless she jumped,' I said.

'Unless she jumped,' said Mike.

* * *

Just minutes after we'd decided I should call Dylan, he called me. I gestured for Emily and Mike to stay quiet.

'Hi, Edie,' he said, sounding more upbeat than I'd have expected. 'How are you?'

'Well, you know. In shock.'

'Yes, as are we all. I'm still with Suzie, and I was wondering if you might be able to pop over?'

'Um, yes. Do you mean now?'

'Well that would be wonderful. Feel free to drive here.'

'Shall I bring the cassette recorder?'

'Yes, please. Oh, and everything else I gave you, if you wouldn't mind.'

'Of course. See you soon.'

'Splendid,' said Dylan and the call ended.

I told the others what he'd requested and Emily looked worried. 'Maybe we should photograph the fake stuff before you give it back?'

'Really?' I asked.

'I'm not sure,' said Mike, rubbing his chin. 'Let's think this through. If Dylan is going to destroy everything and make out he didn't know you before you turned up and murdered Dolores, then yes we should make copies.'

'Cheers, Mike. Like I wasn't traumatised enough.'

'On the other hand,' he added, 'might a record of your undercover role incriminate you?'

'*Us*, surely?' I asked, but he just grinned.

Emily jumped up. 'Hang on,' she said then left the room and ran down the stairs.

Soon she was back, breathless and waving a phone at us. 'My brother's, but we'll need to be quick. Oscar will malfunction without this in his back left pocket.'

'Good thinking, Em,' said Mike, while I went to the adjoining room and took everything from the big cupboard.

Back at the desk, we spread out the bank card, the driving licence, the phone, the cassette recorder, and the opened-up laptop showing Marie Thomas's email account. Emily then took photos, before returning the phone to Oscar and running back up.

'Right!' I said, bundling everything into a bag. 'I'll let you know how it goes.'

They wished me good luck and I walked back home, where I got into my car, lifted the sun visor so I could see the sky, and – just in case I was off to meet two colluding villains – asked my dad to watch over me.

* * *

How odd it felt, turning onto Suzie's drive and parking beside the grey BMW in front of the garage. Dylan's I presumed. Joey's white Audi had gone, exposing a beautiful leafy border adjacent to the house. The one Suzie had been working on. Should I let myself in, I wondered, or ring the bell? Everything felt different, because, clearly, everything *was* different.

The front door was locked, so, using the key I'd been given on day one, I let myself in. I called out, 'Hello?' to no response. The place was a horrible mess, I discovered, as I followed a trail of glasses and plates and discarded party food through to the kitchen, where I caught sight of Dylan and Suzie sitting in chairs on a sunny bit of the lawn.

Suzie waved at me. 'Out here, Marie! Grab a glass!'

But Dylan was already up and coming my way. He stepped into the kitchen wearing a grey T-shirt and gave me a brief, wooden hug. 'Thanks for coming,' he said. 'Can I get you a drink?'

'I did drive,' I told him, 'so perhaps some water?'

He searched unsuccessfully through a couple of cupboards for a glass, then picked up a used tumbler from the table and gave it a soapy wash.

'How's Suzie?' I asked.

He glanced his sister's way. 'You know, it's so hard to tell. I'm not sure how much has registered.'

'Well, I guess that could be a good thing.'

'I'm hoping so. Ice?'

'No thanks.'

'What are you two gossiping about?' called out Suzie. 'Come and get some vitamin B!'

'I think she means D,' said Dylan with a smile. 'She'll be having her siesta soon and you and I can talk then.'

'OK.' I smiled back but felt anxious. 'Is Joey here?' I asked as we walked across the lawn, past the spot where the shoe had landed.

'No,' he said, a bit too emphatically.

I leaned over and kissed Suzie's cheek. She appeared to be in her pyjamas, or perhaps it was a tracksuit. Pale pink and baggy and a little bit grubby. I took the third garden chair. It was wicker and cushioned and as I sank into it and listened to Suzie apologising for the mess in the house, I suddenly yearned for a glass of the wine.

'Actually,' I said, pointing at the bottle, 'I think I would like some. Just a small one won't hurt.' I poured my water onto the grass and held out the tumbler.

'No problem,' said Dylan.

'How are you?' I asked Suzie. Her hair was dishevelled, her eyes were puffy. She didn't look great.

'All the better for seeing you, Marie. It's been a very strange few days, but I'm sure everything will return to normal, once Dolores is back and has cleaned up the mess. Goodness, I have so much to tell you!'

'Really?'

'For the memoir!' She knocked back some wine and giggled. 'Don't tell me you'd forgotten!'

'No,' I told her. 'I hadn't.'

'All about being sent off to boarding school and having to leave my beloved nanny… and Daddy, of course.'

Her brother sighed beside me.

Suzie finished her drink and yawned. 'Marie, did I tell you how I met Pete? In Dereham?'

'Um…'

Dylan made a show of checking his watch. 'Come along then, sis. Siesta time.'

'You could give me a bit longer,' she cried, 'you've only just got me up!' She nevertheless rose to her feet, then grinned at me. 'As the bishop said to the actress.'

While waiting for Dylan to return, I knocked back the wine and then helped myself to another half-glass, and then another wee drop. I'd taxi home and come back for my car when sober.

More than once, I found my eyes drawn to the balcony – God, it was high up – and then to the flat black roof of the gym that Dolores had landed on.

I wondered where Joey had gone, and whether the police had taken the yellow shoe, and if Dylan was going to move his sister-stroke-mother into a home and put the villa on the market. Would the property now be blighted? Of course that might not bother an overseas buyer who'd convert it into flats.

Why was Dylan taking so long? Could I feel his eyes on me?

Never good in heat, and suspecting it was making me paranoid, I took the remains of my drink into the kitchen and made a beeline for the armchair I'd spent most of Saturday evening in.

The aftermath of a party tends to be messy and anticlimactic, but the chaos surrounding me now felt post-apocalyptic. Had the police asked them not to move anything? Unlikely. So why hadn't anyone cleaned up? Perhaps Dylan – 'I'm a well-known restaurateur, you know' – McCrimmon felt it beneath him, and Suzie… well, the only domestic thing I'd seen her do was put freshly cut herbs in a jug.

The front door closing made me jump.

'Sorry!' said Dylan, coming from the hallway. 'Just binning a particularly ripe black bag. Let's move up to the drawing room, shall we? Away from the disarray. You go ahead, and I'll bring us a pot of tea.'

Upstairs was clearer and cleaner, and all looked as it usually did. Apart from the desk, that was. It no longer had a key in either the drop-down lid, or the top two drawers. I pulled at all three and they were locked. Had the police taken the keys? I looked around but couldn't see them, so I sat on the sofa and waited for Dylan.

'I've brought us a slice of cake each,' he said, carrying a large tray with a teapot and pretty cups and saucers on it.

'Great, thank you,' I said, but then to my horror saw two bits of chocolate cake with round-edged shiny brown icing. Just how chunks of a football cake might look. 'But I'm not sure I can manage any right now.' I patted my tummy. 'Big lunch.'

'Ah. Sugar?'

'No thanks.'

I so wanted him to get on with whatever he was going to tell me, but waited while he tipped the teapot, poured and stopped, and then poured milk – 'Say when!' – then handed me my cup and saucer, and then sipped his for a while, before putting down his cup and saying, 'Joey's gone.'

'As in gone, gone?'

'Yes. Taken all his stuff.'

'Do you know where?'

'No. I asked but all he said was maybe he'd find a hotel. I practically begged him to stay. He was in such a state though. Couldn't face being here without Dolores, he told me, then moved his things out after the police had returned for a mid-morning search of the property in daylight. I think they were hoping to find a suicide note.'

'Poor Joey,' I said.

'Poor fucking Suzie, you mean!' snapped a wide-eyed Dylan.

Yikes. Were the staff at *Fabienne* scared of him? I wondered. 'Well, yes… absolutely.'

He took in a deep breath and let it out slowly. A technique for keeping his cool, perhaps. 'We have rather been left in the lurch. I would take my sister to London or Norfolk, if I didn't think she'd be disturbed and disorientated, living in a completely new place. And a retirement home with assisted living is out of the question. I'd have to research and the good ones would have a waiting list. No, Suzie needs to stay here. As for the Dolores thing, Saturday night's drama is already a vague and inaccurate memory for her. However, she isn't quite herself and I'm reluctant to leave her alone when she's been so used to Dolores and Joey being around.'

'Will you advertise for new staff?'

'I already have. But meanwhile I've organised agency care for her, beginning tomorrow. They'll be popping in twice a day, which isn't ideal.'

'No, but OK as a stopgap?'

'Not really,' he said, giving me steady eye contact. 'What would be ideal, is you staying on for a few weeks, Edie. Visiting daily, if possible. You could provide some normality and consistency by continuing with the memoir.'

He waited for a response but all I could manage was, 'I see.'

'I wondered, in addition, if Mike – whom I met at the party and very much liked – might be free to stay in the house. Move in, as it were, for a while. He'd provide overnight security until the carer and cook are vetted and ready to go. And also some evening company for Suzie. He could check the meds she takes, walk her to a restaurant. Obviously, I'd be happy for him to teach his students here, or Zoom with them, whatever. Perhaps you could step in if Mike needed a night off?'

Dylan had certainly thought this through. 'In principle,' I said, 'it sounds doable, although I can't speak for Mike. Of course, if we're doing twenty-four seven we'll have to renegotiate our fee.'

Relief filled his features, his shoulders visibly sank. 'Name your weekly figure and I'll transfer it immediately.'

I reiterated that Mike wasn't yet a certainty, but that I'd let him know. And that I'd be happy to cover some of the night shifts. 'Shall I start tomorrow?'

'That would be wonderful. I've arranged for cleaners to come in but they should be gone by eleven.'

'And do you want me to continue recording Suzie?'

'No need,' he said. 'She does rather tell the same story over and over. In fact, it might be better to get Suzie looking forward, rather than back.'

'Yes, you might be right.' I thought about the last time I'd recorded her, and the tape I'd hidden away in my house.

We sipped our tepid teas for a while, then I felt I had to address the elephant in the room, or maybe it was just inside my head. 'Have the police reached a conclusion?' I asked. 'About…'

'Dolores? Yes and no. I talked to the detective chief inspector today. His team found no evidence of foul play. Every guest could be accounted for, thanks to witnesses, photos and your very helpful footage, Edie. He couldn't say for sure, but unless evidence to the contrary is brought forward, he believes the coroner will decide it was death by misadventure.'

'So it probably wasn't suicide?'

'I think death by misadventure leaves the question of suicide open. But since there was no note…'

'Dolores did cry out, you know. That's unusual in a suicide.'

'Oh, I'm sure it's not that unusual.' Dylan looked at his watch then slowly stood up. 'A change of heart, perhaps, seconds too late?'

I felt I was being given my marching orders, so got up too and followed him down the stairs and out the front door.

'Will you be here tomorrow?' I asked on reaching my car.

'Yes, I will. But if Mike can take over, I'll head off after lunch. Please, both of you, do drive here. It will be reassuring to have a set of wheels on the premises.'

'OK.'

'See you tomorrow, Edie. Fingers crossed Mike will come on board.' He went back to the front door and made sure it was closed. 'I'm popping up to the shops while Suzie's asleep.'

'Can I drop you there?'

'No, but thank you. I enjoy the walk.'

I sat in my car and was about to start it up, but suddenly remembering the wine I'd drunk, and feeling a strong urge to see the balcony again, I didn't. Instead, I got out and walked to the pavement to check Dylan was out of sight. Then, opening the boot, I took the bag of items I was supposed to have returned to him and let myself back into the house. I dropped the bag at the bottom of the stairs and ran all the way up two flights to the back attic room and the balcony, where I whipped out my phone and took photos.

It looked a lot messier in daylight, with four empty beer bottles and two full ones on the floor, alongside the two cushions that had fallen off the chairs Suzie and I had sat on that time – both covered in the contents of a spilled ashtray. And there were tissues, serviettes and other things, including a box of Cook's Matches. On the small round table one wine glass lay on its side. Close to a far corner of the railing was a knocked-over pot of geraniums. Something I hadn't noticed in the dark on Saturday, but I'd check the video later. Could Dolores have tripped over the pot then fallen? The room inside wasn't quite as bad, with scattered books and a couple of food magazines, and the remains of party food on two paper plates. Breadsticks, a grey baseball cap and two lighters. Right, I told myself, after I'd snapped it all, time to get out of here.

When I was halfway down the bottom flight of stairs, Dylan opened the front door, stopped dead, and glared at me.

'I realised two things,' I told him. 'One, I hadn't given you the ID and the recorder.' Now at the bottom of the stairs, I lifted then lowered the bag. 'I also needed to use the facilities.' I pointed, unnecessarily, upstairs. 'And two, I've probably had a bit too much wine to drive. Better to get a taxi and leave the car here. If that's OK?'

'Absolutely.' Dylan smiled and picked an umbrella from the stand. 'It's started to rain. Talk about schizophrenic weather! I'd better dash, Suzie will wake soon. See you tomorrow.'

'Yes,' I told him, scrolling through my phone for the taxi firm, fingers shaking.

SIXTEEN

As it was almost end-of-school time, home wouldn't be conducive to quiet thought, so I bought a flat white and a Danish on the Cowley Road and wandered up to my office with them. As tempting as it was to take a nap in Emily's armchair, or catch up on *The Real Housewives of Orange County, Season 4*, I opened the laptop only briefly to check emails.

I then got out a writing pad and pen. "Pros of me moving into Suzie's for two weeks" I wrote and underlined it. Beneath, I began the list with "Break from family", then, "Give family break from me". I went on to add "convenience", since I'd be going there almost daily, then "very welcome money", and last but not least, that it would be "better for Suzie than having random strangers there".

The "Cons" began with me being "trapped almost twenty-four seven with a woman with mild dementia". I added only one other. "Creepy house where D died – would it freak me out, worsen my PTSD episodes?"

I scribbled down the idea of me doing weekday nights and Mike the weekends, but since he and Seth only had weekends together, either in London or Oxford, that wouldn't work. I drew a line through it and sighed. Exactly when were Mike and Seth going to move their relationship forward? It had been dragging on, part-time, for years now.

A tad hypocritical of me, I realised.

I told myself not to think of Greg and instead switched the timetable around. I'd do the weekends – surely there wouldn't be more than two – and Mike could do three or four overnighters during the week. Or we'd more than likely end up being flexible and just bumbling through it. Although concerned about who'd do the cooking – not my, nor Suzie's, forte – the weekly fee I had in mind would justify having all meals delivered, if necessary.

After asking Emily and Mike to come to the office at four, I had fifty-odd minutes to idle away.

Enough for one episode?

* * *

'So,' said Mike after I'd brought them up to date, 'basically a live-in carer?'

'Well…' This wasn't going well. 'I mean, you could do a spot of gardening too? Cooking? Taking her out?'

'What, to chair yoga?' He laughed. 'The podiatrist?'

'Don't forget the memory clinic,' said Emily. 'Maybe I'll see you there when I take my gran!'

'OK, OK,' I told them. 'Don't worry, Mike, I'll do it. I'll move in tomorrow and be completely tied to a–'

'What are you on about?' he said. 'It sounds fucking brilliant. I didn't get to talk to Suzie one-on-one at the party, but elderly ladies tend to adore me. It's like they pick up on the gay thing, so feel safe flirting with me. When do I start?'

'Oh. Right. Well, obviously, I'd do some overnighters too. But could you manage tomorrow night? Dylan's keen to get back to the restaurant.'

'Yep. And can I volunteer for this coming weekend? Seth and I definitely need some time apart from each other.'

More than all weekdays?

'OK.' I had been half-hoping to do the weekend, visualising Jack staying at my house to help out, and a bit of rekindling going on in my absence.

'You all right, Em?' asked Mike.

'Yeah, yeah.' She corrected her slouch and managed a smile. 'It's just… I dunno, I mean it's great being a mum, but I can't lie, it sort of robs you of your…'

'Money?' said Mike. 'Sanity?'

'More like, self?'

'Maybe you could bring Flo to visit Suzie?' I said, diagnosing FOMO. 'They really hit it off, didn't they?'

'Would that be all right?'

'More than all right. And I'm sure I'll welcome the distraction.'

Mike was chortling again. 'I know. Let's all move in and run the agency from the villa? Dylan or Suzie would pay us more than we'd normally make, and we'd have a posher address than one that begins "Flat A" – in brackets "Above the shop".'

That wasn't our address but I couldn't help liking his idea.

'Flo would have a garden,' said Emily, dreamy-eyed.

'And it's close to my gym,' said Mike.

'Oops!' cried Emily. 'I forgot about Ben!'

'We'll squeeze him in,' Mike assured her. 'Plenty of space. Only bagsy I don't have Dolores's room.'

'Oh, Mike,' Emily and I said, together disappointedly – although I'd been thinking the same thing.

I called Dylan while they were still with me and set out plan A, rather than us all moving in. 'And Mike's happy to start tomorrow,' I added.

'Fantastic. Could you forward me his contact info?'

'Will do.'

After the call, Mike left to pack a bag and postpone the next day's students, and Emily and I carried on chatting for a bit, while I paid a couple of work-related bills.

'What would be really useful,' I said, as she got up to go, 'on top of visiting the villa, would be if you could keep an eye on emails and post over the next week or two? Just a quick pop into the office, every other day, say? You could maybe let prospective clients know we're currently a bit busy but will be in touch very soon.'

'OK,' she said, looking cheerier. 'Yeah, no problem.'

* * *

Alfie burst into tears when I told the kids that I'd be staying at a friend's house quite a lot for a while. Maeve had gone out and I was supposed to be putting them to bed.

'It'll just be a few days and nights a week,' I reassured him, while Betty skipped off. 'And you can FaceTime me whenever you want.' Now I was close to crying. Perhaps the family breakup and the move to Oxford had made Alfie horribly insecure. 'Well, not when you're in the middle of a lesson,' I added. 'Ho ho.'

He laughed too and we had a hug, and before I knew it he was back on the two-screened computer set-up Jack had created, headphones on, happy as Larry and talking to his friends. I'd do something fun with him at the weekend, I decided. He and I could try out ice skating, or visit the alpaca farm, or go back to the maze and not lose each other.

I looked around for Betty to make sure she was OK but couldn't find her. 'Betty!' I sang out to no response. 'Betty?' I tried again from the bottom of the stairs. Was she up there packing me a case?

SEVENTEEN

It was just after three, and although Suzie was chirpy after her nap, it had already been a long day for me. Up at seven to see the kids off to school, cleaning and doing laundry so Maeve wouldn't have to, taxiing to the villa and going over things with Dylan and Mike, eating too many of the sandwiches Mike had gone out for.

We'd agreed we'd both stay over for the first night, while Suzie got used to Mike. My guess was that wouldn't take long, since, as predicted by him, Suzie had gone into flirt mode within minutes of their meeting properly for the first time. 'I'm so pleased you're here!' she'd cried. 'My cotinus definitely needs a man.' Mike had looked understandably alarmed. 'It's a shrub, sweetie,' she'd added, playfully pushing his shoulder. 'I can see what kind of mind you have!'

Dylan had left for London and Mike was currently weeding and pruning out the back. Despite my qualms and nervousness about this new assignment, I felt my eyes grow very relaxed as I sat listening to Suzie's familiar tale.

Suddenly, she stopped talking and looked at me, but didn't seem to be actually looking at me. 'Where's that handsome man you were with?'

'Mike? He's doing a bit of gardening.'

'I'd like to have a quick chat. Shall we take a break and go down?'

I heaved myself up and followed her to the garden, where we found Mike clipping the edge of the lawn with long-handled shears.

'Not too neat!' Suzie shouted as we approached. 'This isn't Hampton Court!'

'Oh, OK.' He stopped trimming and smiled at her. 'Sorry.'

'Mike, sweetie,' she said, 'would you mind helping me move a shrub?'

Her cotinus, I presumed.

'Sure.' He lay the shears on the sharp-edged lawn. 'Where is it?'

'Out the front. Our occasional gardener chap planted it beside the bay window, then Dylan and I moved it yesterday, or was it two days ago… anyway, now I think it should be back in its original spot by the window. Marie, do enjoy a rest in the sun and we'll continue where we left off in half an hour.'

Mike offered her his arm and off they toddled, with me not far behind. The garden was way too hot for resting in.

In the kitchen I slotted our lunch plates and cups and glasses into the dishwasher. The cleaners had done a wonderful job and the house looked lovely again. Since I'd never lived with Mike, I didn't know how house-proud he was, but would no doubt find out. Hopefully, we'd keep it looking this tidy, since the agency staff had been cancelled and there'd been no sight nor mention of a regular cleaner in the time I'd been coming to the house.

I wiped the table and straightened up the chairs, then my eyes wandered to the hallway and Dolores's room. Here goes, I thought, and I went and tried the door. It opened, so I took a couple of wary steps inside.

As expected, it was empty, except for the bed, a desk and chair, the free-standing wardrobe, an ornate mirror above the pretty Edwardian fireplace, and the curtains.

Over lunch, Dylan had told us that Dolores's brother and father had driven down the day before – Monday – and loaded up a hire van with her things. 'The two of them barely spoke to us,' Dylan had said, 'making me feel like an evil rich southerner, who'd exploited their daughter and driven her to suicide.'

'Dolores as much as said she hated her family,' I'd reassured him. 'So I wouldn't take it personally.'

I inspected under the bed and in the wardrobe, which I then wiggled forward and checked behind. On pulling back one of the drawn curtains for more light, there, suddenly, was Mike's face, surrounded by shimmering, deep-red leaves. Suzie was close by directing and pointing.

Back in the kitchen, I had a flashback to something I'd seen in Dolores's room, so I returned and pulled the right-hand curtain to one side. While Suzie waved and I waved back, I picked up the three Scrabble tiles that someone –

the police, the cleaners – had lain side by side on the windowsill. One was an *O*. One was an *E*. The last was a *J*.

'Joey,' I whispered, pulling my phone from a pocket and taking a photo of them. 'Not Lily.'

'I'm going to rustle up a G & T,' announced Suzie, as I closed Dolores's door behind me. She pulled off her floral gardening gloves and changed her shoes to flip-flops.

We all went through to the kitchen, where Mike rummaged through a kitchen drawer and then another. 'Rubber gloves?' he asked Suzie.

She laughed. 'No bloody idea.'

'Ah, success,' he said, waving a pair in the air. From behind Suzie, he then crooked a finger at me and jerked his head in the direction he'd come from.

'Just popping to the loo,' I told Suzie, who was standing with arms on hips and a baffled look on her face as she scanned the room.

'Gin…?' I could almost hear her wondering. I left her to find the ingredients. It would be good for her.

Out front, Mike was kneeling in the right-hand corner of the drive, at the far end of the pretty border, head down, wearing pink rubber gloves.

'What's going on?' I asked, and he got up and pointed.

'This was where the shrub was.'

I peered into the deep dark hole. 'OK?'

'The hole that Dylan dug for Suzie?'

'Got it.' I peered again into the deep dark hole.

'Take a closer look.'

I knelt down and this time saw what appeared to be a brown paper bag right at the bottom. It was ripped, perhaps by Mike's fork. Something yellow could be seen in two or three places, and I felt my eyes grow wide as I looked up at Mike.

'Shall I?' he asked, and I moved out of the way as he reached into the hole. 'It might be nothing but could you take photos?'

While it was still wrapped, and then as he slowly peeled back muddy brown paper, I did as he asked. When what finally appeared was a yellow shoe, exactly like the one that had landed by the cake table, Mike and I swapped 'WTF?' looks.

With the shoe rewrapped and temporarily back in the hole, we sat in my car with the engine on and the AC running. Mike stared ahead while drumming his fingers on the steering wheel. Although it was my car, he'd automatically taken the driver's seat.

'Bit of a long shot,' he said, 'but do you remember if the shoe that landed on the lawn was a left or a right?'

I closed my eyes and visualised it. 'Right.'

'And the one in the hole is a left.'

'It is. But why would Dylan…'

'God knows.'

'OK,' I said, 'let's go back to the event. Dolores jumped from the balcony, or she was pushed from it, and in the process lost one or both of her shoes.'

'Probably.'

I cursed myself for not filming the one on the lawn, but didn't feel like sharing that with Mike. And why hadn't I mentioned the shoe to the police officer who'd quizzed me and asked for my video? Shock, hunger, stupidity? Others must have seen it bounce off the table and land, though. The guests waiting to sing and eat birthday cake. Did one of them pick it up?

'I'm guessing the one in the hole also fell off.'

'Maybe. But more to the point, why would Dylan–'

'Or Suzie.'

'Or Suzie… or both of them, hide it?'

Mike shrugged. 'We need to find out if the second shoe was ever found by anyone, or the police themselves.'

'Without asking Dylan and alerting him.'

'Exactly.'

'Are you thinking what I'm thinking?'

'Ben?' we said together, and I called Emily.

EIGHTEEN

Wednesday brought my first alone overnight stay. Mike had a social event in London that Seth wouldn't let him get out of, but promised he'd taxi back to Oxford if I needed him. I couldn't see why I would but thanked him anyway.

I'd taken Joey's old room, to the right of the front door as you looked at the house. It was pretty and high-ceilinged, with original floorboards and another tiled-surround fireplace. On first seeing the room, the day before, there'd been something of a sad atmosphere still lingering, but once I'd made up the double bed and brought in a colourful rug and a wicker armchair from the garden, then set up my laptop on a small table and added a couple of plants, it all felt cosier.

Mike and I had discovered that Suzie liked to go to bed at eight forty-five and watch a film or TV series on her laptop, until she popped her final pills of the day around ten. 'I'm hooked on US true crime,' she'd told me earlier, when I'd gone in to wish her goodnight. 'Small-town America does murder so well, don't you find?' I'd agreed and she'd recommended a series.

Around half ten I peeked in to check she was asleep, and she was. I then took a quick shower, went around and closed and locked all windows and doors and switched off lights. Dylan had said to leave the landing light on in case Suzie ever began wandering. Her bedroom had its own en suite, so she was unlikely to emerge before morning.

Once in bed with my phone, I went back to the notes I'd begun earlier:

> *Why was Dolores's shoe in the hole wrapped in brown paper? Was brown paper, as opposed to a*

plastic bag, used because it would lead to faster decomposition of the canvas shoe?

Police unaware of either shoe, according to Ben, who'd accessed the police report, rather than asked anyone. Emily didn't tell Ben anything about either shoe, or about her premonition.

One idea – could Suzie have crazily insisted they bury a single shoe of Dolores's in memory of her? Perhaps she'd found it, say in the garden, the morning after the party… Worth asking S?

I was beginning to feel nicely tired and relatively relaxed after an active day. Before he'd left, Mike and I had taken Suzie out for lunch in trendy Jericho, and then we'd walked back via Port Meadow, the area of common land and water meadows that isn't far from the city centre but feels like real countryside. Twice during the walk, Suzie had complained of a headache she'd had for days – 'Possibly weeks' – and once back home she'd fetched me a piece of paper listing her medications beneath the name, address and contact details of her GP. 'I always see him,' she'd said. 'Would you mind calling the surgery for me?'

"Make S a doctor's appt." I added to my notes, as my eyes grew heavier and I began to feel sleepy. It felt a little early to drop off, so I got my laptop from the table. I considered, then ruled out *Buried in the Backyard* – recommended by Suzie – and opted, of course, for *The Real Housewives*. One episode would be a well-deserved treat after the past couple of days.

I woke up with my headphones still in but no sound coming out. The episode had finished, the screen was black and the room was in total darkness. Having moved the laptop to a safer part of the large bed, I tried to go back to sleep, but an annoying scratching and scraping noise prevented me from doing so. *Scratch, scratch, scrape, scrape.* It stopped briefly, but then started up again.

The sounds were definitely coming from the front drive that my window overlooked. Oh Jesus, had Dylan returned under cover of darkness to dig up the yellow shoe? I couldn't go to the window and look in case he saw me. *Scrrritch*, I heard again, and my insides tied themselves up. What would happen when Dylan didn't find it? He'd know we had it. Would he let himself in and throw me off the balcony?

'Dad?' I whispered, looking up. 'Help?'

Reaching for my phone, I first turned down the brightness, then tapped on a contact.

'Hey, Edie,' said a groggy-sounding Greg. 'Booty call?'

'It could be,' I said very quietly. 'In fact, yes.'

'You coming to me, or me to you?'

'The latter. I'll text you the address.'

'Now I'm intrigued as well as horn–'

'Be quick!' I whispered and hung up.

Woodstock, to the north of Oxford, wasn't far from Suzie's house, and knowing Greg was on his way gave me the courage to open the heavy curtains an inch. Sadly, all I could see was my car parked inconveniently close to the window. I considered standing on the chair for a better view, but what if I fell off and cried out? *Scratch, rustle, scrape, scratch*, I heard again.

I shivered, pulled a jumper on over my T-shirt and shorts, and crept to the kitchen-diner, where I sat holding my phone in one hand and a bread knife in the other.

* * *

I'd never been so happy to see Greg, or in fact anyone.

'Do you want to put that down?' he asked, while I hugged him in the open doorway, standing on tiptoe to look over his shoulder.

'Oh yeah, sorry. I was just… slicing bread.'

He shut the door behind him, then I relocked it and we went through to the back room, where he sat at the table and I hovered nearby.

'Edie, are you all right? I've never known you cut bread in complete darkness.'

I switched on a lamp and put the knife back in the drawer.

'Or want sex quite so badly. What's going on?'

'Nothing,' I said. 'Ha ha, nothing. Nothing at all.'

Greg pulled a sceptical face. He was looking really good, even for him. Really, really good. But wait, was his hair beginning to thin on top? I rarely saw him from this angle, but the lamplight was showing up definite patches of bare scalp. Could it be the start of a slippery slope for him? Christ, I hoped so. Then we might end up like Plain-Jane Eyre and rugged, handsome Rochester, who could only feasibly marry once he was blind and disfigured.

'Oh yeah,' said Greg, 'I think a fox has been at your compost bin. There's a horrible mess on the drive.'

'Oh dear…' I looked up at my dad and smiled, then took an opened bottle of white from the fridge and led Greg to my room.

'Cute outfit,' he said from behind.

'Thanks.'

NINETEEN

At ten forty on Thursday morning, Suzie and I were in the waiting room, in a surgery to the north of Summertown. Suzie's usual doctor had retired, however, 'Dr Elsie Ford could squeeze her in this morning,' I'd been told on the phone, and I'd said yes, great.

Someone called Elsie would be either twenty-something or a hundred-and-twenty-something. I was hoping for the former. Young female GPs were the best listeners and the quickest to refer you to a specialist. Plus they never sighed, scowled or harrumphed when you added four more ailments to the original. In my experience.

Suzie had initially been thrown. 'Retired? But I adored Lawrence! We'd exchange dirty jokes and he'd gossip about his other patients. I always left laughing.'

After Suzie was called in, I texted Emily to see if she wanted to bring Flo over once her shift in the shop ended. "No longer working in shop," came her reply. "Flo at new childminder this afternoon so can we come soon?"

I said yes and to just turn up.

Was this good or bad news? I wondered. Emily was knackered – true – but her shifts had got her out of the flat and interacting with people. Was she pregnant, as I'd suspected at the party, or had she just been tuning in to negative energy in the villa?

I scrolled through the local news – something I did several times a day – and yet again found only the original article reporting Dolores's fall. And a Google search for her name brought up nothing. Not even a Facebook page or other social media. Since my impression of Dolores had been that she was super private, this came as no surprise.

'Marie?' a woman was calling, and I realised she meant me. I held up my hand and went over to her. She had waist-length red hair and wore colourful leggings with Dr. Martens. 'Are you Suzie's carer?' she asked.

'I am.'

'Would you mind coming through and joining us? I'm Dr Ford, by the way.'

She led me down a short corridor and into her room, where Suzie was buttoning up her top.

'Everything OK?' I asked, taking the seat next to her.

'Fit as a fiddle!' declared Suzie.

Dr Elsie pulled a piece of paper from a printer. 'I've done an appraisal of Suzie's medication and made some adjustments.' She handed me the new list. 'As you can see it's a little shorter.'

It was, in fact, a list of one: "Amlodipine 5mg per day".

'For blood pressure. Down from 15 milligrams,' explained the doctor. 'Suzie's blood pressure was very low, and could have been causing the headaches. And you're going to try to taper off both the antidepressants and the sleeping tablets you have left, aren't you?'

'I'll try my very hardest,' Suzie told her.

'Perhaps you could support her with that, Marie? Start with half the usual doses, then after one week, a quarter, and so on. Oh, and do check Suzie's blood pressure every day for a while. You can pick up a reader in any chemists, and here's some info about BP readings.' She handed me another piece of paper. 'Suzie appears to have done very well since her second hip replacement two years ago, and so I've taken her off the co-codamol painkillers. And also the statins, since her cholesterol never was high. Do you have any questions?'

'Are you saying Suzie's been taking unnecessary medication?' I asked. 'Quite a lot of it, for quite a while?'

The young doctor coloured up. 'I certainly felt a review was overdue.' It was probably as close as Elsie could get to calling her ex-colleague a lazy fuckwit. She smiled at Suzie. 'If your headaches continue, do come back and see me.'

* * *

While Suzie was taking a nap, Emily and Flo rolled up, and the four of us were now at the table eating a healthy pasta dish Mike had made. It wasn't at all bad and even Flo was wolfing it down.

'You love broccoli, don't you, Flo?' said Emily.

'Bockly,' said Flo, reaching for more. 'Uh sushi?' she added, looking around.

Wow, I thought. Maeve would only eat jacket potatoes at that age.

'She's upstairs having a little sleep,' Emily said. 'She'll be down soon.'

Ah, Suzie not sushi. 'That's sweet,' I said. 'That she remembers her.'

'Yeah, she was like Sushi this and Sushi that after the party, then the penny dropped.'

Mike, who'd been distracted by emails, finally put his phone down. 'Listen, how do you guys feel about reaching out to Joey? Maybe we could talk him into coming back? I mean, as much fun as this is, I do have fish to feed.'

'I dunno,' said Emily. 'It might be a bit soon? For Joey, I mean.'

I helped myself to more pasta. 'On the other hand he could be feeling excluded, or that no one cares about how he's holding up.'

'If we do reach out,' said Emily, 'I don't think we should tell or, like, involve Dylan.'

'Christ, no,' said Mike. 'Do we know Joey's surname?'

I had a think. Had I seen any letters to him? 'No,' I said, 'but Suzie might.'

'Shall I call him now?' I asked and they both nodded. 'I think he blocked Suzie, but he hasn't got my number. Only my fake one.'

I tapped on his name and his phone rang several times before I was diverted to voicemail. 'Hi Joey,' I said. 'It's Marie here. I was really sorry to hear you'd left Suzie's and have been a bit worried about you. Hope you're OK. It would be nice to see you, so if you feel like meeting up do call me on this number. Take care.'

'Sushi!' Flo cried, bouncing up and down and pointing at the stairs.

'Is that darling Florence?' asked Suzie when she reached the bottom. 'I thought I heard you! Listen, I've got a little something I've been keeping especially for you.'

She came and scooped up Flo and carried her over to the nearby Welsh dresser, where she opened one of the drawers and took something out. 'Isn't it fun?' she asked, dangling Dolores's bracelet from a finger.

TWENTY

After a nine-hour uninterrupted sleep in Joey's room, I sat in bed with a coffee and planned the day. Mike would be arriving to do the weekend shift late afternoon, so I hoped to do a bit of recording with Suzie in the morning, then walk with her to a café in Summertown for lunch. Maybe a potter in the garden after her siesta. But when I took her a wake-up cuppa, Suzie had other plans.

'I barely slept,' she croaked, 'and I'm feeling a little unwell, to boot. I think it might be flu.'

'Oh dear,' I said, guessing it was withdrawal, since I'd already begun reducing her meds.

'I'll spend today resting, Marie. Would you mind bringing me my meals?'

'Not at all.'

'A fry-up would be fabulous. Lots of protein.' She shivered in her nightie then reached for a shawl and wrapped herself in it. 'Scramble the eggs, won't you? I can't abide them boiled. Had a nasty experience with one, which I'll tell you all about when I'm…' She slid under the duvet, turned on her side and moaned.

I thought of returning some of the half-tablets I'd taken out of her organiser, but couldn't decide if that would make me an irresponsible carer, or a caring carer. Perhaps I'd leave it up to Mike.

* * *

After a long day of tidying, reorganising the fridge, lunching alone and reading, I filled Mike in on the pill and BP regime, and the bracelet Dolores had claimed she never took off.

'Perhaps the paramedics removed it?' was his first suggestion. 'Or it fell off when she…' was his second.

'Good thinking,' I said, hugely relieved that I didn't have to distrust Suzie.

After giving Mike a quick demo of the blood pressure reader, I drove off, via the ring road, to the east of the city and the Scholar, where I'd arranged to meet Astrid for a quick drink before going home. I sat on one of their wobbly chairs and listened to her tales of woe. How all job vacancies were dull-sounding and underpaid, and how she regretted her choice of divorce lawyer.

Then at one point she said, 'Over your left shoulder at two o'clock. Turn slowly and let me know what you think.'

I wondered what had happened to the footballer, Jake, but did as she'd asked. 'Green trousers and a wedding ring?'

'Damn.'

'Kidding!'

'Really?'

'Yeah, they're olive not green.'

'Hilarious, Edie.'

She was hard to do humour with but it was fun trying. 'And don't you have to be eighteen to get married?'

Astrid screwed up her eyes for a better short-sighted view, while I told her – among other things – about Mike and me standing in as carers until Dylan found replacements for Dolores and Joey. I resisted a second drink, as I wanted to catch the kids before bedtime, but Astrid went for another glass of wine.

Back at the table she asked me for Dylan's number.

'Now he *does* have a wedding ring,' I warned her.

'Christ, not my type and way too old. But that fabulous house of Suzie's, over on the right side of town? That I do fancy.'

'Don't tell me you're–'

'Yes, Edie.' She knocked back some wine, then smiled to herself. 'I'm going to apply for one of the positions.

Cook, I think. Then I'll let my house, and Jakob and I will live relatively cheaply at Suzie's. She does like children, I believe? There'll be good schools and more importantly, richer men in the area.'

'Very good,' I said. Had she finally got the hang of joking? 'And Maeve could rent your house, ha ha.'

'Perfect!' she cried, holding up a hand to high-five me. Another thing I'd never known Astrid do. Perhaps she'd had a little smoke before coming out.

'Now,' she said, 'about this buried yellow shoe.'

'Yes?'

'It's an odd thing for Dylan to have done. Why not stick it in a black bin bag with household rubbish, take it to a tip and chuck it in a massive communal skip. Never to be seen again.'

'Maybe he was planning to do something like that but didn't have time before the police arrived on Sunday morning.'

'So why didn't he dig it back up before leaving for London?'

'Because… I don't know. He might have thought it was as good a place as any, and he wasn't to know Suzie would move the shrub back to its original spot.'

'And you haven't thought about going to the police with the shoe?'

'Obviously we've discussed that, but as far as they're concerned it wasn't a suspicious death. What if we open a can of worms and end up with some crazy scenario in which Mike and I are implicated?'

Astrid shrugged. She'd said all she was going to on the subject, I could tell, and her eyes roamed back to Olive Trousers.

'I'd better go,' I told her. 'You coming?'

'I think not.'

I didn't hug or kiss her goodbye, because it wasn't her thing, but I did stop beside her prey. 'My friend wants to know if you'd like to buy her a drink.'

'Really?' he asked, scoping the room. Too late, I spotted the wedding ring he was tugging off.

'On dear!' I said, not wanting to be that kind of wing woman. I pointed vaguely across the room. 'Wrong man! Sorry!'

At home I unpacked my small case, shoved things in the washing machine and read two books to the kids; one chosen by each of them. After Betty fell asleep during Alfie's choice, he and I whispered about our Saturday ideas, deciding in the end on a cathartic revisit of the Blenheim maze. Betty had a friend's birthday party in the morning, so she needn't know we'd gone without her.

Downstairs, Maeve asked if she could pop out to see a friend for an hour, and I said no problem, then took a novel she'd recommended up to my room. Partway through chapter one, I heard the ping of a text. It was from Dylan.

> *Coming to see Suzie on Sunday, early afternoon. Hoping both you and Mike could be there for a chat? I'll be driving down from Norfolk, so do save me some lunch! Dylan*

I replied saying yes I'd be there, and yes to his lunch request. Then – with my head full of Dylan, the shoe, Suzie's baby and the falling Dolores – it took me a good three hours to go off to sleep, shortly after Maeve arrived home and tried, unsuccessfully, to creep up the stairs. In my head, she'd been to see Jack.

TWENTY-ONE

Mike and I had hoped for sun, but Sunday turned out to be dull and overcast. While Suzie remained in her bed, still unwell, he and I went ahead with our plan and set up four garden chairs and a small table on the drive, in front of the garage I hadn't yet been in.

'You know Suzie has a Mini in there,' I told Mike. 'Says she can no longer drive it because angry men beep her.'

'No, I didn't know that. Is there a key somewhere? Wouldn't mind checking it out. And perhaps there'll be some more-useful garden tools than those in the shed.'

We went and checked out the dangling keys and found a likely candidate. It worked, and when the metal garage door creaked open we were greeted with a very clean-looking white Mini that Mike worked out had a 2016 registration.

'Nice,' he said before inspecting the rear half of the garage, where he got quite excited by an enormous cardboard box of old toys.

I went and had a poke around with him. There, all muddled up together, were metal soldiers and tanks and ships and guns, and train tracks and train carriages and little wooden houses and shops. People and farm animals also tumbled around as we rummaged. On the side of the box someone had written "FOR DYLAN", and I wondered if it had been passed on by Suzie's philandering dad. I also wondered how much lead I was touching.

'Seth would love this,' said Mike. 'In a previous life he definitely had a train set in the attic.'

Realising the time, we locked up the garage, washed our hands thoroughly, took the chicken out of the oven and, as Dylan's latest ETA approached, settled into our front-drive seats with our mugs of coffee, ignoring the gathering clouds.

On his arrival, Dylan swung into the drive at some speed and just managed to avoid mowing us down. Almost as speedily, he then reversed out and parked in a two-hour space. Something told me he'd be one of those men beeping his sister.

'We thought we'd sit out here in the sun,' explained Mike, as Dylan approached carrying flowers. 'Only now it's disappeared.'

'Yes, Suzie and I have often sat on the front doorstep in the late afternoons. Listen, I'll just pop these in, say hello to her and then I'll join you.'

When he was out of earshot, Mike turned my way. 'He didn't look at the cotinus,' he whispered.

'He didn't,' I whispered back. 'But was that a deliberate tactic?'

'Plan B?' asked Mike, and I nodded.

'I'm going to check the potatoes,' I said at normal volume.

'Make sure you chuck a cup of salty water over them and turn the oven up ten degrees?'

'Will do,' I said, but didn't. They looked perfectly fine. I took them out so they wouldn't overcook, but left Mike's secret-recipe gravy simmering.

'Ah, a roast!' boomed Dylan behind me. 'Still a favourite in my restaurants.' He had a wan-looking Suzie on his arm. 'We think the virus is on its way out, and that a glass of white wine might completely see it off.'

'I'm sure it will,' I said, gathering four glasses plus the bottle from the fridge. 'Come and sit in the…' I was going to say sun '…front, Suzie.'

'Don't mind if I do,' she croaked.

I followed them out and helped her into the chair that Mike and I had allocated for her, should she appear. This meant Dylan was sitting with his back to both locations the cotinus had been in. I watched him carefully without staring, and not once during our superficial ten-minute conversation did he turn and look at the border.

Finally, Mike said, 'Suzie, did you tell your brother we moved the shrub back to its original place by the window?'

'Er, no I…' said Suzie, while Dylan didn't flinch, gulp, or spin his head around to look.

Instead he tutted and chuckled. 'I told you it would just get lost in that spot, Suzie. That it was better by the window.' He leaned over and squeezed her hand. 'You silly goose, as Mummy would say.'

Either he was one cool customer, borderline psychopath, or he had no idea the shoe had been in the hole.

'The shrub seems to have settled in pretty well,' I said to Dylan. 'When was it first moved?'

'Sunday morning. It was a good distraction for us while we waited for the police to come.'

'And Joey was still here then?' asked Mike.

'Yep. He was allowed to leave once the search was over. Listen, I hate to be pushy but my breakfast was five hours ago.'

Mike and I apologised profusely and we all went in and enjoyed the roast, although Suzie flaked out partway through and returned to her bed. We filled Dylan in on the medication problem, but played it down somewhat, so he wouldn't feel guilty for taking his eye off that particular ball.

Over dessert, he told us he'd be back later in the week to carry out some interviews, and to show the short-listed applicants around.

'Oh yes, Edie, that reminds me. A woman called Astrid something gave you as a referee. Apparently, she's worked as a consultant on your cases? She claims to be an amazing cook who specialises in Scandinavian cuisine, but can turn her hand to anything. So, basically sounds perfect. Are you happy to vouch for her?'

'Um...'

Had he forgotten they'd been introduced at the party? He'd been grumpy at the time, or distracted, so perhaps she'd made no impression. Something I'd probably not share with her. I needed to stall so asked who'd like coffee. Dylan declined, as he was heading off asap. Mike didn't respond at all, so busy was he wringing his hands – or Astrid's neck. Or mine.

After saying goodbye to his sister, Dylan thanked us for the meal – 'Great roast potatoes!' – and disappeared.

Once we'd filled the dishwasher, Mike and I sat down opposite each other at the table for a quick post-mortem. I was going to head home soon and Mike was kindly covering till Tuesday morning, to make up for me missing my Sunday.

'OK,' I said, 'let's work through the shrub-moving process. Dylan would have dug the new hole first, presumably?'

'It would make sense. Then he'd have gone and dug up the shrub and carried it across to the new hole.'

'Leaving the original hole unfilled for a bit while he replanted the cotinus.'

'Which could have taken a good five or ten minutes, what with Suzie giving him directions, followed by filling in, bedding in, watering and so on.'

'And during that time he'd have mostly had his back to the original hole.'

'He would,' said Mike.

'Giving someone the opportunity to pop Dolores's wrapped left shoe in the empty hole, then throw some soil in to cover it. Perhaps brown paper was used because it would blend in.'

'Can you imagine Suzie going to all that trouble?' Mike asked.

'I'm not sure.' I shared my theory of Suzie burying the shoe to commemorate Dolores's life. 'However,' I added, 'if Dylan had helped her do that, he'd surely have mentioned it today. Asked if you'd come across it when you redug the hole.'

'I agree.'

'So,' I said, 'we're back to square one… but not quite.'

'Joey?'

I nodded. 'Joey.'

As I made moves to leave, Mike's demeanour changed and he threw me one of his disapproving scowls.

'Yeah, yeah.' I sighed. 'But honestly, Mike, how was I to know she'd apply for Dolores's job?'

TWENTY-TWO

Just after nine on Tuesday morning, as I was taking things out of my boot on Suzie's drive, Mike appeared and gestured for me to get back in the car with him.

'OK, first off,' he said, once inside, 'I can't find Suzie's pill sorter thing. When I asked her where it was, she said she'd put it away for a rainy day, but wouldn't tell me where.'

'Oh dear. Well, I'll try and find it.' Luckily, I'd taken all her boxes of tablets to my house, while we'd been cutting her doses. 'At least we can set up another one.'

Mike stared at me in an odd way. 'The thing is, we might not need… Look, come and see for yourself.'

I locked the car and we both carried my things into Joey's room.

In the kitchen sat Suzie, typing on a laptop. 'Morning, Marie!' she said, briefly looking up at me. 'Excuse me whilst I get all this down.'

'Suzie's writing her autobiography,' Mike told me. 'She kindly let me read a little and it's very good.'

'Yes?' I asked, but got no signal that he was joking and it wasn't just nursery rhymes and shopping lists.

He nodded at me, wide-eyed. 'Walk me out to my car? Bye, Suze!'

She stopped and blew him a kiss, then went back to battering her keyboard, like it was an old sit-up-and-beg typewriter.

'She did an hour in her gym,' Mike whispered out by his car, 'between six and seven, then made us both a cooked breakfast, then began writing around eight.'

'She actually cooked?'

'Yep. It's weird, I mean she was in bed completely exhausted most of yesterday, then stomping around and agitated in the evening, searching for something. And now she's sort of…'

'Normal?'

'Yes, normal. I mean, if I hadn't been here all night, I'd swear Suzie's twin had replaced her.' He checked his phone. 'Shit, teaching at ten. Er, good luck?'

'Thanks!'

* * *

I picked up the three pages Suzie had printed out for me. She'd known not only how to work the printer, but how to send the printer a document. 'Thanks,' I said. 'Is it saved in–'

'The cloud? Of course.'

I put the kettle on for an instant coffee, but when Suzie saw what I was doing, she came over. 'Come along, Edie. Let's make a proper one.'

Edie?

She smiled. 'I've heard Mike, Dylan and little Flo call you that. Do you prefer it to Marie?'

'Actually, I do. Marie's my middle name and I tend to use it professionally.'

Suzie plugged in the Nespresso machine and took two pods from a box. 'I do so love writing,' she sighed. 'However…' She took out two coffee cups I'd never seen and gave them a rinse. 'If I'm to continue with the memoir, I'll need to track down Caro. I have old contact details for her grandparents in my address book, which Daddy had written down when Caro came to stay. It's probably of no use now but worth trying. The trouble is, I can't find the bloody thing.'

'The address book?'

'Yes. It was always in the same place in the bureau and now it isn't. I hunted everywhere last night.'

It was actually outside in my car, in the space where the spare wheel lived. 'I'll have a look for it too, shall I?'

'Would you mind? Milk?'

'Yes please.'

I thought we might sit and chat over our coffees, but Suzie settled back at her keyboard. 'Oh yes,' she called out, as I took mine to drink in the garden while I read her pages. 'If I can't track down Caro myself, we may have to resort to getting help. You don't know any private investigators, do you?'

I stopped, went cold, looked back at her merrily typing and quickly convinced myself she hadn't found me online.

* * *

She'd started at the very beginning with her conception in a flat over a fish and chip shop in Ripon, Yorkshire. By the end of the four pages, she was living in a small cottage in Norfolk and being looked after by her paternal grandmother while her mother toured. Suzie wrote well – there went my ghostwriter job – and I looked forward to reading more. However, when I went back in to encourage her to carry on with it, she was in my party armchair, staring into space and looking glum.

'Suzie?' I said. 'Are you OK?'

'I'm missing Joey, that's all. And he won't answer my calls, the naughty boy. We've always been remarkably close, right from the start, so how could he disappear like that? I'm wondering if he went to his mother's place, up in Leicester, but her address is in that damned book. When they first arrived, I asked both Joey and Dolores to give me a next of kin to contact in case of emergency.'

"A's Mother" I remembered, written at the end of the A section. I had a photo of it in my phone but could hardly show her.

'I don't suppose you have Lily's phone number?'

'Oh, good thinking!' She reached for her mobile and scrolled through her contacts. 'No. No Lily.'

'Do you know the name of her catering company?'

'I'm afraid not. Let me look online.'

I watched her go to Google and type in "Lily catering Oxford" then scroll through the results. Nothing.

'Right!' I said. 'You get back to your very engaging memoir, Suzie, and I'll search every nook and cranny for the address book.'

'Thank you, Marie. I mean, Edie!'

I made some noise searching my room. I then rummaged through the credenza drawers in the hall, then slipped out to my car. I popped the still-chocolate-milk-ruined book up my jumper and went upstairs to search the drawing room.

Where was the best place to 'find' it? Somewhere that would explain the brown-liquid damage. 'Aha,' I said, suddenly inspired.

Down in the kitchen, I held it up. 'Is this it, Suzie? I found it upstairs, behind the large plant pot beside the bureau. It looks like someone has been over watering the plant and–'

'Yes!' cried Suzie, taking it from me. 'You clever thing! Oh but…'

'Yeah, some of the pages are stuck together. But here, let me see what I can do.' I held out my hand and she passed it back. 'It's Caro you want to find details of?'

'And Joey's mother. Bless you, Marie. Edie. You're a star!'

In Joey's room I scrolled through the photos I'd taken and wrote down "Annie Reeves" followed by a landline number. And then I copied down the 1960s landline number of Caroline's grandparents. They'd have been long gone, but it was a starting point.

Before lunch, which was warmed-up leftovers of Mike's tray bake, I took Suzie's blood pressure. I wanted to make sure it was low enough to endure a spike when she called the numbers I'd written down. Her BP was normal, and after unsurprisingly having no luck with Caro's grandparents' number, she tried Joey's mother, who picked up and caused Suzie to throw her phone my way. 'You do it?' she whispered.

'Is that Annie?' I asked. 'Joey's mum?'

She said yes, but that she was driving and late for an appointment, and was Joey all right. I reassured her, then said we were trying to get in touch, as he'd moved out and left a couple of things behind.

'Typical Joey,' she said, chuckling. 'You could try his dad? I can't look up his number or send it right now, but I can give you his address.'

'That would be useful,' I said, then grabbed a pen and newspaper and wrote down the address she reeled off.

'Sorry, have to go, bye,' she said, before I had a chance to ask Joey's father's name.

'He lives on the other side of Oxford,' I told Suzie, turning the paper round for her to see.

'Sixty-four Flowerdown Avenue, Rose Hill, Oxford,' she read out. 'Let's drive there?'

'Do you mean now?'

'Goodness, no. I need to work on this all day.'

No siesta? Damn. I'd always savoured those two hours off. Was new Suzie going to be hard work, and if so how would Astrid cope? Since she'd clearly been unhappy about her current job prospects, house, neighbours and bank balance, I'd reluctantly given Astrid a glowing reference.

* * *

After a light lunch, Suzie cleared the table, then sat back at her laptop. 'Perhaps we'll go tomorrow afternoon? I'll take Joey his favourite chutney from that Summertown deli.'

'OK. But remember he's probably staying somewhere else. With Lily, or at a friend's.'

'I know, but his father might point us in the right direction.'

'True.'

I couldn't help wondering if Suzie's new vitality and clear thinking would gradually fade away, like it did with those old people in that film I couldn't remember the name of. I hoped this wasn't the gods playing a practical joke, and that it really had all been her incompetent GP's fault.

I loaded the dishwasher, moved laundry from washer to dryer, then went to Joey's room and took Suzie's nap for her.

TWENTY-THREE

Early Wednesday morning, I called my office landline to pick up any messages that might have been left.

'Hello, Fox Wilder,' I was told. 'How may I help you?'

'Em?'

'Oh, Edie. Hi.'

'You're in the office, then?'

'Yeah, been, like, manning it, while you're away.'

'So you're really no longer working in the shop?'

'No, I'm not. Ben reckoned it was the job that was making me sad, so we found Flo this brilliant childminder, literally around the corner, and I'm looking for something else. I might as well be here, as in the flat. Oh, yeah, and I got us another case. Been following this woman whose boyfriend thinks is a hooker?'

'And is she?'

'Hundred per cent. Got photos and even a recording of her haggling over the price.'

'Please be careful, Em.'

'Yeah, yeah.'

I couldn't quite believe this. On the other hand I could, Emily had shown initiative in the past. 'Sorry to ask, Em, but you did get a contract signed by the client?'

'Course. I charged him double the usual because he was such a knob.'

A little questionable but I told her she'd done well. We talked about Flo and her new childminder for a while, then when Suzie swanned down the stairs on her way to the gym, I ended the call and flagged her down.

'Morning, Suzie. Do you still want to go to Rose Hill later?'

'Absolutely. Let's have lunch en route?'

'OK.'

* * *

We stopped in Summertown for Joey's favourite chutney, then throughout the journey across town Suzie sat in the back of my car typing away on her laptop. In Iffley, not far from Flowerdown Avenue, I managed to prise her away from her *magnum opus* to have a pub lunch. Once we'd ordered, I began to prepare her for a very different Joey.

'If he's there, he may not be too welcoming,' I warned her. 'It could be that he's depressed about Dolores and needs time alone. You mustn't be upset if he says no to coming back to the villa. In the meantime your… Dylan appears to have found some great candidates for the cook and carer positions.'

Suzie looked up from her notebook, pen poised. 'How do you spell fuchsia?' she asked, shaking her head. 'It's completely gone.'

I googled it and told her.

What might be better use of my time, I realised, was to prepare Joey for a very different Suzie. I took my phone outside and tried him twice, but he didn't answer and I didn't leave a message. Just turning up was beginning to feel like a bad idea, and I was definitely jittery. If I hadn't wanted to find out how Joey was myself – and, who knows, maybe discover why he buried the shoe – I might at this point have taken the distracted Suzie to the wrong address, then home again.

But I didn't, and just after two o'clock we pulled up outside an attractive 1920s round-bay-windowed semi with an attached garage and a pretty front garden. Suzie snapped her laptop shut and I grabbed the jar of chutney.

'Ready?' I asked her.

'Before we go in…'

'If anyone's home.'

'Indeed. I was just wondering if I should offer Joey a pay rise? If that would entice him to return?'

I thought of the art deco chair and the treadle sewing machine. No, she absolutely shouldn't.

'Worth a try,' I nevertheless said, whilst suddenly feeling the need to let Mike and Emily know where I was. I shot off a quick message with the address added, then saw Suzie was back on her laptop. The woman was obsessed.

'Ready?' I asked again, and when we got out of the car I handed her the jar. At the door, with a feeling of impending doom, I banged the small brass knocker.

'Another cotinus!' said Suzie. 'Look.'

I turned to see the shrub she was pointing at, and when the front door opened we both had our backs to it.

'Hello?' came a voice that wasn't Joey's. 'Can I help you?'

Spinning around, I faced a tall slim man with curly white hair.

'Hi,' I began.

Suddenly Suzie gasped like a drowning woman coming up for air, dropped the chutney on the path and said, 'Peter?'

'Suzannah McCrimmon?' asked the man. His knees buckled and he clung to the door frame. 'Good grief!'

Suzie opened her mouth but nothing came out. Her face was ashen, her bottom lip trembled.

'Could we come in?' I asked before one of them dropped dead. I wasn't feeling that steady, myself. Joey's dad was Peter? Who was also – although we didn't know for sure – Dylan's father?

'Yes, please do.'

I picked up the chipped jar and followed the two of them into an open-plan living room and kitchen.

'Take a seat,' said Peter, his voice shaky. 'What a shock you've given me, Suzannah. Shall I put the kettle on?'

I plonked myself in a leather armchair while Suzie followed Peter to the kitchen, where she finally found her voice. 'Do you have anything stronger?'

'I do. What's your tipple?'

'Alcohol?' she said and they both laughed.

'Red wine?'

'Perfect.'

'What can I get you?' Peter called out. 'Sorry, I don't know your name.'

'It's Edie. A coffee would be lovely. White, no sugar.'

'Coming up!'

I sent an update to Emily and Mike with many exclamation marks, then perused the bookshelves beside me. Plato, Val McDermid, Naomi Klein, Chomsky, John Locke, Jane Austen, travel books, quantum physics, several noir crime novels, Emily Dickinson and Ian McEwan. I couldn't read the top-shelf titles but they looked more academic.

'Here you go,' he said, putting a mug on the coffee table. He went off and returned with twinkly blue eyes and a plate. 'And here are a couple of cookies I made earlier. Salted caramel and pecan.'

'Ooh, thank you.' I took a bite of one and went straight to heaven. 'Delicious!' I called out, and he gave me an endearing salute. If Suzie didn't rekindle things with Peter, I'd snap him up myself.

They came and joined me, sitting side by side on the sofa and clinking glasses.

'Well,' Peter said, 'where shall we begin? I mean, what brought you both here?' He was nicely spoken, but not super-posh like Suzie.

'We were hoping Joey might be here,' I said.

'How I miss him,' said Suzie. 'And not just for his margaritas.'

'He left very suddenly on Sunday,' I told Peter, 'and didn't tell Suzie or her brother where he was going. We're a bit worried about him.'

Peter looked bemused. 'I didn't know you had a brother, Suzannah?'

'Oh. No, of course you wouldn't. He came along after… you and I… after I left, you know.'

'I see. And how do you know Joseph? Joey.'

Now Suzie looked bemused. 'He's lived with me for over two years, as my assistant. I had health issues and Dylan found me some wonderful helpers.'

Peter got up and paced around, running a hand through his white curls. 'As far as I know, Joseph's been a live-in carer for a woman called Dierdre.' He looked at Suzie. 'You don't sometimes go by Dier–'

'Certainly not.'

Peter chuckled. 'No,' he said, then sat down again. 'This is all very odd. Joseph isn't staying here. In fact, I haven't seen him for months. I suggested meeting up for his birthday, but he had some ghastly flu bug.'

I willed Suzie not to mention the party and it worked.

'How extraordinary,' she said, 'that you haven't seen one another when you're in the same city.'

'What do you mean?' Peter asked. 'My son lives and works in Bristol.'

I felt I was in one of those sci-fi novels, where someone shifts into a different version of the world. In this case, a dimension in which Joey lives in Bristol and

Suzie never got dementia. Would I go home and find I had more children?

'Dierdre's family advertised for help,' continued Peter, 'what, two years ago? Joseph applied and was taken on.'

'Definitely in Bristol?' I asked.

'I've never been to Dierdre's place, as she's wary of strangers. But Joseph and I meet up in Bristol two or three times a year, and he sometimes visits me here.'

'How very odd,' said Suzie. 'Unless Joey has managed to juggle two old biddies!'

'You're far from that,' Peter told her.

'I was just fishing,' Suzie said with a wink.

'Have you met Lily?' I asked Peter.

'Who?'

'Joey's girlfriend?'

'I haven't.' He shook his head. 'My son has had a number of girlfriends. Some I've met, others not. He didn't mention anyone last time I was in Bristol.'

'Do you mind me asking when that was?'

Peter took a sip of his wine. 'Let me think. Yes, of course. It was on my birthday.'

'The fourteenth of March?' asked Suzie.

'Golly, you remembered.'

When they went back to flirting, I looked around the room. It was cluttered, but with attractive and interesting things. Deep-seated orange sofa with geometric cushions, and the old leather chair I was in. A saxophone and three guitars propped in a corner beside two shelves of record albums. Colourful masks hanging on one wall and an African fabric covering the dining table. It was a mini, more ethnic, version of the villa.

'You have a very nice house,' I told Peter. 'Have you been here long?'

'Thanks. Sixteen years. I came back to Oxford following my divorce, shortly after Joseph left for Bristol University. Just a thought but he might be at his mum's?'

'We've spoken to her and she hasn't seen him. She gave us your address.'

'Ah.'

'And are you in good health?' asked Suzie, rather randomly. Although a standard topic, I guessed, for folks their age.

'Physically, yes. However…'

Suzie, rather shockingly, put her hand on Peter's thigh. For all we knew there could have been a wife or girlfriend in the picture, about to walk in. 'Have you had emotional issues?'

'Nicely put,' said Peter. 'Let's just say I never quite got over something that happened in my teens.'

'Me?' she asked.

'Yes.'

'I'm so sorry, Peter, but it was out of my hands and I had no way of contacting you and it was sheer bloody agony for me.'

'Did you have our baby?' he asked, his eyes reddening, his hand now on top of hers.

'Yes, I did,' she said. 'A little boy. But how on earth did you know about that?'

'I worked it out. That you were pregnant. And there was some talk amongst your school friends. What I never knew was whether you'd gone ahead with having the baby.'

'I'll tell you more later,' said Suzie. 'It's complicated.'

Peter sighed. 'My poor Suzannah.'

Both of them were tearful now and they moved in for a hug. I felt I should leave them alone but was glued to the leather chair. It was quite a drama and I had a front-row seat. And cookies.

I waited for them to end their cuddle, then said, 'Does Joey know?'

Peter nodded. 'I had a spell of heavy drinking, actually several over the years. And during one, it all came out, unfortunately. Joseph didn't take it well. He had a sibling

I'd kept secret from him. "Maybe," I kept telling him. "Maybe not." How I wished I'd never mentioned it. The demon drink, eh?'

'But you're OK with it now?' asked Suzie, pointing at his glass.

'I'm in a happy place,' he said, 'so it's not a problem. I had a relationship end earlier this year, and expected to plummet and hit the bottle, but I was fine with it. Aging has some pluses.'

'You're still the sixteen-year-old Peter to me,' said Suzie. 'Tell me what you did, after I left. You were at the boys' grammar, I remember.'

'You really want to know?'

'I do.'

'I fell apart, to be honest. Did so badly at my O-levels that they wouldn't let me into the sixth form.'

'Oh, Peter.'

'And so I ran away to sea. Merchant Navy. Had a great time, seeing the world, working my way up to chief officer.'

I thought of Dolores, and how she and Peter might have shared maritime stories.

'A girl in every port?' asked Suzie.

He laughed. 'That's for me to know. Anyway, approaching forty, it all began to pall and I felt the need to catch up on my education. I met someone, much younger, and we married and had Joseph. However, my being a perpetual student with part-time jobs meant money was always short. I ended up with a doctorate but no proper career path. Plus an unhappy wife and a child who constantly asked for things we couldn't afford. Games consoles and the trainers his friends had. I'd feel like a failure and hit the bottle. I'm sorry, is this too much?'

'Not at all,' said Suzie. Her eyes twinkled just as Peter's had. Star-crossed lovers came to mind and I prayed he didn't currently have a partner.

'And how about you, Suzannah? Tell me about your life.'

Unable to listen to it again, I excused myself. 'Just going to walk off the yummy cookies,' I said, but I wasn't sure either of them heard.

* * *

'Peter, you must come back with us,' Suzie said, when I started hinting that we should leave soon. One, we'd been there two hours and I was getting hungry, and, two, I was tired of playing gooseberry. 'Now I've found you I'm never letting you go!' she added.

Words many men might not welcome, but Peter beamed at her and said, 'Ditto!'

From that, I presumed there wasn't a current squeeze in his life.

The two of them sat chatting in the back of the car, and I tried not to eavesdrop. At one point, though, I caught Suzie saying she'd recently met this amazing astrologer, who'd told her an old flame would come back into her life. Mystic Emily, presumably.

On walking through the front door, Peter took in the hallway. 'My, Suzannah, you did do well. If only I'd pursued Sandie Shaw or Lulu instead of going to sea!'

He had an infectious laugh, as well coming across as all-round nice. Although, who knew who Peter became when drinking heavily.

We decided on Chinese food. I ordered a hefty delivery and set the table for four. No mention had yet been made of Dolores, and although I felt Peter should know why Joey had left so suddenly, I was reluctant to bring it up in front of Suzie, just in case it burst her happy bubble and set her back. I'd needed to pry the lovebirds apart, somehow, so before leaving Rose Hill I'd gone outside and called Mike.

'I'll be there in an hour,' he'd said, after we'd discussed what and what not to tell Peter. The 'what not' was about

Dylan being passed off as Suzie's little brother. It wasn't our place to tell Peter, and more importantly it hadn't been verified.

The food and Mike arrived at the same time and after the two men were introduced, we dug in. The table talk was of 20th-century social history – Peter's field – and English tutoring – Mike's field – and being a rock star's common-law wife – not mine, obviously. I stayed quiet, mainly because I wasn't too sure who I was. Detective, ghostwriter, carer… The roles were definitely blurring, not helped by the rather good cocktail Mike had thrown together. 'Thank YouTube,' he'd told us, when we'd praised it.

But then Peter said, 'What's your story, Edie? How did you end up in this line of work?'

Which line of work? I told him about my late father having been a police officer, and that I'd been considering following in his footsteps, but managed to get a place at Oxford. 'My sister had just graduated from Oxford, when I started.'

'What a clever family you are,' said Suzie.

'However,' I continued, 'I very uncleverly found myself pregnant at the end of the first year, and dropped out. It was a random hook-up at a ball, and I didn't very much like the chap.' I left it at that.

'He was an arsehole,' said Mike, almost under his breath.

'And did you have the baby?' asked an intrigued Suzie.

'Yes. My daughter Maeve.' I got out my phone to show her pictures. 'And these are her children, Alfie and Betty.'

'Gosh, how gorgeous they are. Do you mind me asking what their heritage is? Joey would always tell me off for asking that in restaurants and at parties. "I'm just interested," I'd tell the waitress or the new academic neighbour.'

'No, I don't mind. My daughter is part Spanish on her father's side. Alfie's dad is South American, and Betty's father is British and white, as is my mum. She lives with my sister Jess in Australia. No children but lots of dogs.'

'You must miss them?' asked Peter.

'I do, but we Zoom, and we fly back and forth.'

Mike offered to make coffee. Here, finally, was my opportunity to divide the lovers.

'Suzie,' I said, 'there's something I need to go over with you, upstairs. Could we just…' I stood up. 'It won't take long.'

'Oh, OK.' She squeezed Peter's shoulder and told him not to go anywhere.

'As if,' he said and they kissed. On the lips.

I was amazed at the speed of this reconciliation, and could only assume it was an age-related limited-time thing. Or was it that Swinging-Sixties promiscuity never left a person? I tried not to think of them having sex, just as Maeve was initially creeped out by Greg and me. 'Really?' she'd asked, the first time he'd appeared for breakfast. 'Here?'

I nodded at Mike and he nodded back, and as I rounded the corner to the stairs, I heard him tell Peter about the box of 'boys' toys' he'd found in the garage. Would he like to see them.

Once up in the drawing room, I had to think on my feet. 'Your medication,' I said. 'Mike told me you've hidden it?'

'No,' Suzie said with a smile. 'I know where my tablets are, therefore they're not hidden.'

'But you are taking the amlodipine?'

'Yes, I am.'

'Would you mind if I checked your blood pressure? The doctor did say…'

'I know, I know.' She got up off the sofa and took the BP reader from a shelf. 'Here. I've been doing it twice a day.' She showed me the screen and clicked back through a series of perfectly good readings.

'Excellent,' I told her, then racked my brain for another pretext.

Suzie leaned in. 'There is something we could do, whilst up here.'

'Yes?'

'Put fresh sheets on my bed?' She bobbed her eyebrows at me. 'Think I might get lucky tonight.'

A text pinged through from Mike. "Done" it said.

TWENTY-FOUR

On Thursday, Dylan was due at half ten to carry out interviews. He'd asked for me to be in on the selection process, but I'd planned to slip away before then and have Mike take my place. I really couldn't interview Astrid.

Peter had indeed stayed the night. In Suzie's room. Since I had no idea if she'd been completely candid with Peter regarding Dylan, I didn't want the two men running into each other. So, after explaining over breakfast about the candidates coming to look around, I booked Peter a taxi, making sure we swapped contact details before he left. I said to call me if he heard from Joey, or just felt like a chat.

'That's very kind of you,' he said with a smile. 'It's been a lot, as they say.'

When the taxi arrived and Suzie swooped in for one last snog, I went and tidied my room for the upcoming house tour. Things got thrown in the wardrobe and the bed got neatened. I gave the room a dust and a polish and added one more plant from the kitchen-diner. On the marble mantelpiece above the fireplace, I propped up a couple of arty photos from the entrance hall. Then, after a thorough hoover of the floor and rug, I saw I'd missed four calls from Peter. Had he left his house keys here? There were two messages and I tapped on the first.

'Edie, it's Peter. Could you ring me as soon as possible? Thanks.'

I tapped on the second, left three minutes later.

'Sorry to ring again, only my house has been wrecked. Completely bloody trashed.' His tone was less friendly, more frantic. 'I want to call the police… but I… well, I'm worried Joey might be behind it. Not that he's ever done anything like–'

I didn't listen to the rest but immediately called him and said I'd come straight over. I told him not to do anything or touch anything, and to definitely not tell Suzie. 'See you in twenty,' I added and he gave me an emotional thank you.

When I called Emily, she was in the office. 'I wouldn't mind a bit of support,' I told her. 'Mike's going to help vet the applicants here at the house. Astrid could be one of them, so I recused myself.'

'Probably for the best,' she said. 'Mike'll make sure she doesn't get the job.'

I explained everything in a couple of sentences, then gave Emily Peter's address and said to text when she arrived. Since strangers were coming to the villa, I packed up my laptop and a couple of other things I wouldn't want nicked, and put them in the car. Then, up in the drawing room where Suzie sat typing at the open bureau, I said goodbye and good luck to her. 'I hope you find the perfect cook and carer.'

She stopped typing and looked up. 'I don't need anyone bloody caring for me, although a cook-cum-cleaner would be most welcome.' She went back to her screen, fingers poised.

'One thing, Suzie.'

'Yes?'

'I think it might be better not to mention Peter to Dylan. Not just yet?'

'Don't worry, Edie. I've already decided to keep mum.' An unfortunate choice of word, but I nodded my approval. 'As I did for decades with regards to Pete and me, after my divorce.'

Why had I worried? Suzie excelled at keeping secrets. At the door, I turned around. 'Any luck finding Caro?' I asked.

'Dead,' she said, touch-typing away.

* * *

It certainly was a mess.

'Nothing's broken or missing,' Peter told me. 'And thank God they didn't destroy my vegetable patch. That would have been the last straw.'

I could tell Peter was all at sea, but resisted giving him a hug. He definitely looked older and frailer than he had first thing, when he and Suzie had walked down the stairs – hand in hand, smiling and glowing.

I stood in the living room and took it all in. Books lay on the sofa and floor, the musical instruments were on their sides, ornaments and vases were overturned. At the kitchen end, the scene was even worse. Pans and crockery all over the floor, along with the contents of the fridge and freezer. Every plant on the windowsill had been tipped out of its container, leaving soil everywhere.

'And upstairs?' I asked.

'The same.'

A text arrived from Emily, saying she was outside. Since Mike had explained to Peter about Fox Wilder being employed by Dylan, and why, I was able to tell him my fellow investigator had come to assist and we went out to meet her.

As we approached the Golf, Emily stepped out in a fitted dark-grey skirt suit and pale-cream silky top. She wore subtle make-up and her hair was in an intricate version of a French pleat. When she held out a hand, Peter shook it.

'I'm sorry to hear about your house,' she said, then strode ahead of us on small-heeled investment-banker shoes.

'You OK?' Peter asked me.

'Um... yes. Yes, yes.' We followed Emily – once an undereducated drug addict, now an *Apprentice* finalist.

'Lovely cotinus,' I told Peter.

'Isn't it?'

* * *

I drove the three of us to a café off the Iffley Road. It was mid-morning, so the place was empty enough to talk openly over our drinks.

'She looks adorable,' Peter was saying to the photos Emily was swiping through.

She chuckled. 'These are funny. Look. Suzie took us to her garage and gave Flo some dressing-up costumes that used to be Dylan's.'

'Oh, ha ha, wonderful!' cried Peter.

'She doesn't even know what a Native American is, but looks great. Her favourite is the policeman costume. Her daddy's a police officer. Oh and here she's a cowboy. It's way too big for her.'

'What a delightful little girl,' said Peter. It was probably a welcome distraction for him, but we needed to discuss the house trashing.

'Does Joey have a key?' I asked.

'He does.'

'And what are your thoughts, Em?'

'Um...' She slipped her phone in a soft black leather handbag. 'At first, I thought it was someone who was angry. But an angry person would probably have broken things. I reckon it was someone looking for something.'

'It couldn't have been your ex-girlfriend?' I asked Peter. 'Come back to get something?'

'I doubt it. We had an amicable parting and she went home to Ireland. She's also something of a neat freak.'

'OK.'

Peter put his head in his hands for a while, then looked up at us. 'I've just had a thought. In all the excitement, and what with the wine, I might not have closed the bathroom window yesterday. It's on the side of the house and an average-sized, relatively fit person could climb onto the flat roof of the garage and clamber up and in through that window. I know that because I've done it, although not for a while. Damn. I've been meaning to replace it with a smaller, safer window for years.'

'We'll check when we go back,' I said, but Emily had her eyes closed and was holding up a palm for us to be quiet. 'It's open,' she told us. 'Definitely.'

'Photographic memory,' I explained to Peter.

He looked relieved. 'So it might not have been Joseph, after all?'

'Um,' I said, pretty convinced it had been.

'If it was Joey,' Emily said in a quiet, gentle way, 'can you think of anything he might have been searching for?'

'Nope. I honestly can't. Oh. Unless…'

'What?' I asked, maybe a little too desperately. Emily gave me a please-go-to-the-loo side-eye and head tilt, so that was what I did.

* * *

'They've gone,' Peter told us, back at his house.

He was holding the tiniest of plastic storage boxes, one that you could fit maybe three grapes in. Some bits of tape dangled from it.

'What have?' I asked.

'The keys. I taped this to the springs of the guest bed, thinking he would never find it, what with all the board games and Christmas decorations stored under there.'

'You mean Joey?' asked Emily.

'Yes.'

'And what are they the keys to?' I asked.

'Rosebud Cottage,' he said.

I began clearing the sofa of books so we could at least sit down while we were pulling teeth, then crossed the obstacle course to the kitchen to see if I could find Peter a tot of something to loosen him up. A bottle of whisky lay on the floor, and on the counter was a chunky glass. Perfect. I half-filled the glass and handed it to him on the sofa.

'Take your time, Peter,' said nice-cop Emily.

'But do drink up!' I added with a quick smile.

He knocked some back, pulled a face, shuddered and coughed. 'Rosebud Cottage,' he rasped. 'Just outside Henley. Belongs to Joseph's mother, Annie, who inherited it from her parents. She couldn't bring herself to sell it, and it's provided her with rental income during times I wasn't being a great contributor. About eight years ago, it became a holiday rental. And, well, let's just say that Joseph, knowing he'd inherit it one day, has regularly put pressure on her to make it over to him while he could do with some financial stability.'

'Do you think she will?' I asked.

'For a while she seriously considered it, but then a young family turned up there one Saturday, having booked it for a week, and found Joseph and his friends in residence, off their heads on drink and drugs, telling them to eff off.'

'Ooh, not cool,' said Emily. 'Poor family.'

'We've kept the keys hidden from him since then. As it's close to Oxford and Annie is in Leicestershire, I occasionally go and do a bit of painting and grass cutting. Pruning the roses.'

'I take it you're not going to report this?' I asked.

'I'd rather not.'

'In that case, we'll help you tidy up.'

'Goodness, that would be very kind.' Peter finished his whisky and looked Emily's way. 'Although I'm not sure you're dressed for it?'

'Come to think of it,' I said. 'Why *are* you dressed like Meghan Markle in *Suits*?'

Emily smiled at me. 'I think you'll find, Edie, that Meghan almost never wore a jacket in that series. Watched every episode.'

'You're being evasive,' I said, eyes narrowed. 'Do you think we should up our game, dress-code wise?'

'No. OK, maybe a bit. It's just that I had a job interview today. Only then you called and needed me, and I thought, do I really want to be a receptionist for a firm called Cistern Solutions on some, like, business park miles from Oxford, or do I want to carry on earning peanuts with Edie?'

I felt myself bristle. I paid Emily twice the minimum wage, whether she did anything or not. The trouble was, since Flo's arrival, she'd only been able to set aside a few hours a week for Fox Wilder. 'Let's have a chat about it, Em? Sometime soon?'

She nodded. 'Sorry about the peanuts, Edie. You're dead generous.'

'I know I am.'

'My gran used to tell me I opened my mouth and let my belly rumble.'

We laughed, then from behind Emily came the sound of gentle snoring. How sweet Peter looked, his head on a book. I removed the empty glass from his hand and whispered, 'Shall we start with the kitchen, Em?'

By the back door, she yanked off her shoes and groaned. 'How can women wear these things?'

'No idea. You look hot in the suit though.'

'That's what Ben said, before we went upstairs for a qui–'

'Counters first?' I jumped in. 'Or floor?'

'As he only had ten minutes.'

Floor, I decided.

* * *

Mike rang when we – Peter included – were halfway through tidying the living room. Apparently, Dylan had decided to stay until Saturday, giving us two nights and a day off. This was definitely good news as I was exhausted, and after a couple of weird days, it would be lovely to do normal for a while. Emily, Mike and I decided to meet in the office at eleven the following day. Emily and I would hear how the interviews went and Mike would be told about the missing key.

When the living room looked as good as it could without a dust and hoover, Peter assured us that he'd manage upstairs himself. Before leaving, I got the address of Rosebud Cottage from him – 'Just in case' – and shared it with Emily and Mike.

* * *

Back at home, I dumped my things, hugged the kids and put the kettle on. Maeve and I caught up over a cuppa, then after an early dinner, I read Betty stories in bed, arm around her. She was very sweet and chatty, then finally fell asleep. Perhaps I'd grown on her.

Downstairs, the three of us decided to watch a film.

'You choose,' Maeve told Alfie, and he went for *Shrek Forever After*.

Maeve lit some candles and we watched the film, laughing when Alfie did, feet up on poufs and a cosy fleece over our six knees. Halfway through, we stopped for a loo break and Maeve microwaved popcorn. It was such fun, that I couldn't for the life of me understand why I'd hoped they'd move out. Did I really want to go back to letting myself in with a leaden heart? Microwaving a lamb hotpot for one?

On the other hand – I was now recalling – I'd absolutely loved my independence. My downtime. Having Greg over for a weekend, instead of mainly going to his.

When *Shrek* finished, Maeve swept up popcorn and I led a sleepy Alfie upstairs to bed, skipping the teeth-cleaning bit. I too was ready for bed after all the tidying and cleaning at Peter's, but downstairs I found two glasses of red wine on the island, and Maeve seated on a stool, looking tense and pouring cashews into a bowl.

'What?' I asked. 'What's happened?' She'd dropped out of the course? Had she and Jack got back…? No, no, I'd given up on that dream scenario.

'Do drink some, Mum,' she said, pushing my glass towards me as I mounted a stool. Half of her wine was already gone. 'Are you sitting properly? On that stool?'

'Yes.' Please don't let her be ill, I prayed. Ditto the kids. And Jack.

I took a couple of gulps, and one more, while Maeve threw a nut in the air and caught it in her mouth.

'I've found Jesus,' she said.

TWENTY-FIVE

'So…' Mike was sitting in Emily's orange chair, legs stretched out. He'd been to the gym and looked sickeningly healthy. 'Lots to discuss. Shall I start with the interviews?'

'Yeah, OK,' said Emily. It was good to see her back in Camden Market clothes. Maybe.

'Difficult,' he told us, 'hostile and embarrassing. And that was just Suzie.'

I laughed. 'I'm not surprised. She seemed dead set against having another carer.'

'Yep. On top of that, she took a shine to Astrid.' Mike grinned at us. 'Initially.'

'What happened?' I asked, grimacing.

'OK, so Astrid started well. She looked great and said lovely things about the house and garden, pointing out her favourite flowers and climbers – "Oh, a herb patch, how perfect" – that kind of thing. Towards the end of the interview she reeled off a list of Scandinavian fish dishes, pickled and whatnot, that she loved to make or buy. Then when Suzie interjected and told her she wasn't a fan of fish, and rarely ate it, Astrid berated her and said, wait for it… "No wonder you have replacement hips!"'

When we'd all recovered and I was wiping away tears, Mike told us that another person – a very nice guy – had been offered the job of cook. 'He starts next week.'

'Well, that's something,' I said. 'And maybe Suzie won't need a carer, now she's recovered her, um…'

'Brain?' suggested Emily.

She and I then told Mike about Peter's wrecked house, and the missing set of keys to Joey's mother's cottage.

'I wondered what that Rosebud Cottage text was about,' said Mike. 'So, let's just go through what we know, and whether we think we should pursue anything further, since no one's paying us to. Have we still got the plan of Suzie's house?'

'In the cupboard next door,' I told him, and he went and got it and nailed it to the wall, plain side out. He said next time he'd bring his mini flip chart. 'Or perhaps we should invest in one?'

'Noted,' I told him. 'Shall we start with Joey?'

'And his odd behaviour?' asked Emily. 'Like telling your dad you live in a whole other city?'

Mike wrote "Joey" on the card, then "Odd behaviour" then "Lying about Bristol".

'Possibly stealing things from Suzie,' I said.

'Also, not asking his mother if he could use the cottage but ransacking his dad's place for the key?'

'And,' I chipped in, 'deserting Suzie so soon after Dolores died. It seems out of character.'

'But do we really know anyone's true character?' asked Emily, enigmatically.

I shook my head. 'I'm not sure we do. I mean look at… No, I shouldn't say.'

'Come on,' said Mike.

'It's just that… oh nothing.'

'Stop being a tease, Edie.'

I laughed. 'I haven't heard those words for decades. OK, I was going to say, I think I prefer the old Suzie to the one that doesn't have… you know.'

'Dementia?' asked Emily.

'I prefer to think of it as temporary medically induced brain fog. There's clearly nothing wrong with Suzie's brain. But she's less warm now. More self-contained and dismissive.'

'I agree,' said Mike. 'However, she is distracted by – or should I say laser-focused on – the book. Which isn't a bad thing. Not if it makes her some money.' He looked back at the list. 'Any more odd Joey behaviour?'

'Lurking?' I suggested.

"Lurking", wrote Mike. 'And the biggest odd thing of all, guys?'

Emily tapped her chin with her phone. 'That he was working for his dad's first girlfriend?'

'Give yourself an A star!' said teacher Mike.

Obviously I too had thought that was a strange coincidence.

We worked our way through Dylan and Suzie fairly quickly, then when Mike took down the list and put it away, Emily and I looked on my phone for a flip chart to buy. I left her to choose one and order it on my account while I nipped to the loo to sort out my hair and put make-up on. I'd had a text from Greg earlier saying he'd be free all afternoon if I fancied doing something.

Back in the office, Emily handed me my phone. 'It's arriving Monday. Listen, I've got to head to the childminder's now, sorry. Meeting my mum and dad there to introduce them and show them the ropes. I'll need their help when I get a full-time job.'

Ouch. I couldn't stop Emily moving on, but didn't want her to, obviously.

'So, what's next, Edie?' asked Mike. 'You'll cover Saturday night after Dylan leaves?'

'OK.'

'And I'll take over Tuesday morning?'

'That works for me.'

We all left the office together and Emily hurried off and Mike asked what I was doing for the rest of the day.

'Well, I'm going to do a food shop and then we've got Jesus coming for dinner.'

'That sounds pretty huge. Oh, wait. What? Not *the* Jesus?'

I nodded. 'Heyzoos.'

'Will Alfie be OK?'

'Out of my control.'

'Jesus,' said Mike. 'I mean…'

TWENTY-SIX

Walking back towards home and my car, I pulled up the text I'd got from Greg earlier.

"How about a trip to Henley?" I replied.

I got a thumbs up.

"Meet at Heyford Hill Sainsbury's at one?" I suggested. That way, being closer to the store, I could grab a few items for supper before he got there, and he could leave his car there for three hours. Perfect. Another thumbs up arrived, and I was reminded of how easy-going Greg could be.

* * *

He found me as I was loading up the boot with enough for the disciples, should they turn up too.

'Mine or yours, or two cars?' he asked.

'Mine?' I suggested. 'Save the planet, and if we break down we won't starve.'

On the way to Henley, I first of all told him the latest Joey happenings, and that he could well be living in Rosebud Cottage. I hadn't yet mentioned Dylan being Suzie's son. Allegedly.

'And you want to see him, why?' Greg asked.

'Well, we're all a bit worried about him, and also Suzie's missing him and won't countenance another carer.'

'Right. It won't take long, though?'

'Not at all.'

I told him I had Heyzoos news too. Greg had been around for years and knew the story of Alfie's conception.

'So, apparently, Jesus was recently in Greece and recognised the woman behind a bar as someone he'd met when travelling nine years ago. She and Maeve had travelled together for a couple of months before coming across Jesus, and then the two girls stuck together for the rest of Maeve's trip. The friend, now in Greece, told Jesus about Maeve having been pregnant with his child, and that Maeve had tried contacting him via the email address he'd given her, but her messages had bounced back.

'It's a mean trick,' said Greg. 'Like one digit wrong in the phone number.'

I gave him a look.

'Yeah, yeah,' he said. 'Guilty.'

'So…' I continued, 'unbeknownst to me, Maeve met up with Jesus in London a few days ago, so she could check him out. Apparently, he works at various jobs in Cartagena, saves up, travels and repeats. Still single, and still devastatingly attractive. It's true, she showed me a photo.'

'Does Jack know?'

'He does, and he's also coming for supper.'

* * *

As we approached Henley, I said, 'Could you keep an eye on your Google map? Or switch Lolita back on?' His chosen GPS voice hadn't sounded old enough to walk herself to school, let alone navigate for us.

'In seventy-five yards, turn right.'

This I did, then we drove around half a mile to a pretty hamlet.

'You have reached your destination,' said our guide.

I thanked her and let her get back to the classroom, then with the engine still running, I read through the names on the row of cottages beside us.

'It's there, I think,' said Greg, pointing across the road to a big tree with a gate beside it.

I could just make out "…bud Cottage".

'Good.' I turned off the engine. 'Listen, Joey doesn't know you, so would you mind nonchalantly wandering past to check it says "Rosebud"? I'm not sure I want him to see my car.'

Greg took a deep breath. 'OK, Edie, now I'm feeling uneasy. Last time I was caught up in one of your cases, someone punched me in the face.'

'Yeah, sorry about that.'

'When you said Henley, I pictured lunch in a riverside restaurant and a stroll past George Harrison's place.'

'We'll do those later. Promise.'

Greg groaned and got out. With his head down, he sauntered along the narrow road, looking at his phone. God, he was attractive. He took his time, then finally turned around, crossed back to my side and slid into the car. 'Rosebud Cottage,' he confirmed.

'OK, so I'll go and knock on the door. If I'm not back in say ten minutes, I'll text to say I'm all right.'

'And if I don't get a text?'

'I don't know, Greg. You could use your gumption?'

'Haven't got any. Ran out. I've been meaning to buy–'

I went in for a long kiss, which shut him up and hopefully made him think I'd be worth saving.

* * *

There was no doorbell, and there was no knocker. It took several rounds of me banging my knuckles before the door opened a few inches, and there was three quarters of Joey's face. He was pale and dazed-looking with dark circles under his eyes.

'Marie?'

'Hi, Joey.'

'What are you doing here?' His voice was quiet rather than confrontational, and I began to relax. 'How did you find me?'

'I er… Look, can I come in?'

'It's a shithole,' he said, grimacing.

'No problem, I live with young children.'

'You do?'

'Lots to tell you, Joey.'

The door opened onto a room that fitted his description. 'Maybe we should go in the garden,' he said, leading me down a corridor, past a kitchen and bathroom, and out onto a patio with rattan garden furniture on it. He'd lost weight, I noticed.

Joey sat in a chair, then his eyes bounced left and right several times and he jumped up again. 'Er, would you like a coffee?'

'Maybe some water?'

'Coming up!'

The garden was unexciting but nice enough. It could have done with Peter giving it some TLC. Was that a cotinus? Something I hadn't heard of a week ago was everywhere. As I waited, I checked my phone for messages, scrolled through the news headlines and looked at recent photos of the family. I wondered how the whole Jesus thing was going to play out. My greatest fear, of course, was that Alfie would be taken out of the country by his father, never to be seen again. I shook that scenario out of my head and wondered why my glass of water was taking so long.

About to go and check, I saw a cross-looking Greg approaching from the side passage, followed by Joey.

'We have to go,' said Joey. 'Your car can't be outside my house.'

'Why not?' I asked.

'We'll take it to where I park mine. Come on.'

At this point, Greg and I could have run, jumped in the car and gone to Woodstock for a nice cuddle. But Joey said, 'Please? There are things I need to get off my chest and I'm so pleased it's you, Marie, who's turned up to hear them. But we can't stay here.'

He smiled for the first time, and what with the compliment and his apparent desperation, not to mention the worrying thinness, I said, 'OK,' and Greg said, 'Bloody hell, Edie,' and Joey said, 'Edie?' and I said I'd explain later.

After locking up, Joey followed us to my car.

'It'll be easier if I drive,' he said.

'Sorry, but no,' I told him firmly.

He sat in the back and directed me along more narrow winding roads for about a quarter of a mile, then onto a farm track.

'It's part of that barn,' he told me. 'You can park the car to the left and it won't be seen from the road.'

I parked and we got out and Joey took us around the front of the barn and through a small door within the large main door. There was a bit at the bottom that we had to step over. He switched on a dim light and there in front of us was a large wooden room, or perhaps a small barn, containing Joey's car and nothing else. The place was hot but had a damp smell, and shards of sunlight came through gaps in the roof and walls. Joey left the door open, presumably for more light and air.

'I've got two fold-up picnic chairs,' he said, opening his boot. He passed one to me and another to Greg. 'They're actually Suzie's but don't tell her.' Joey himself sat sideways on the car's passenger seat, facing us, door wide open.

'Who are we hiding from?' I asked.

Joey shook his head. 'I can't tell you. Sorry, Marie. Or do you prefer Edie?'

'Edie. How have you been?'

'Not great. I take it you found my dad?'

'We did, via your mother. You gave Suzie her details as your next of kin, then your mum told us your dad's address.'

'And Suzie remembered doing the next-of-kin thing?'

'She did.' I summarised Suzie's journey from over-medicated to writing her own memoir, and caught Joey welling up.

'That's so tragic,' he said, 'but also heart-warming.'

I agreed. 'She misses you, which is one reason I'm here.'

'I miss her too, and the house. And poor Dolores.'

'I know.'

Greg put his hand up, and we looked his way. 'I don't know about you guys but I'm ready for lunch. Shall I go and get us some food and drink from your car, Edie?'

'Good idea.' I took the key from my pocket and explained to Joey about the grocery shop I'd done.

He held out a hand. 'Leave your phone, would you, mate?'

'Sure,' Greg said, with a quick smile. He was dealing well with a tense and bizarre situation, and I loved him for it. Unless, of course, he was about to drive off and leave me at the mercy of someone who may or may not have pushed a woman to her death.

He was soon back with the kids' small cartons of juice, sourdough rolls and three bananas, and we all dug in. Somehow, having a little picnic together changed the atmosphere. Diffused things. Even Greg looked cheerier. Did people still make banana sandwiches? I wondered. Such a good combination.

'Right,' said Joey, 'I'm going to start at the beginning.'

'Fire away,' I told him.

'I didn't have the easiest of childhoods...'

Oh right, that far back. Luckily, the camping chair was quilted and comfy. I slotted my carton into its drink holder.

'There was never much money around, and on top of that my dad, Peter, went through bouts of depression and heavy drinking. His father, a bank manager, had been a bully, so I put it down to that. I was always scared of my grandad, so felt some sympathy for Dad.'

I nodded, mouth full.

'Then one time, when Dad was off the wagon, and I was old enough to join him in the pub for a half pint... I think I was fifteen, so not legally old enough. Anyway, he started talking about when he was my age and at the grammar school in Oxford, and what he and his friends had got up to, including meeting girls from the posh boarding school. Then he talked about one of them called Suzannah, his very first girlfriend, and things got a bit graphic because he was so pissed. Although I wanted him to stop, I was also gripped, you know?'

I nodded again.

'He and Suzannah would regularly meet up, and were head over heels in love, and one thing led to another, i.e. sex. And then one Saturday she didn't turn up, and the next week she didn't turn up either, and my dad was so upset and tried to find out what had happened from some of the other girls, and one said the rumour was that Suzie was pregnant because she'd been throwing up and had gone off her favourite pudding.'

'Poor Peter,' I said.

'Dad went off to sea for twenty years and put it out of his mind, but when he came back and married a woman he didn't really love – my mum – it hit him again. He tried looking up Suzie, with no luck, and assumed she'd married and changed her name. When we had that talk in the pub, sixteen years later, he said he couldn't bear to dig it all up again, investigate, whatever. Not after so long. So I decided I'd do it, when I was old enough. I'd find Suzannah.'

'And you did,' I said.

'It took some doing, but yeah. Got myself into her life, kind of in disguise, as a handyman's sidekick. Long dyed hair, baseball cap. She and I hit it off, and at some point, when she was finding it hard to walk, I sowed the seeds of her maybe hiring a carer, and why didn't we see if I could get the job.' Joey smiled. '"Our little secret," she'd said. With the help of some ace references, written by friends, I did get it.'

'Did you know Dolores at that time?'

'No, she got the cook position all on her own. Anyway, Suzie never mentioned having had a kid, and would always clam up if I asked her about her teenage years. So about a year in, I put the autobiography idea to her. And then again, and again. I offered to help her write it, and that triggered Dylan to find her a ghostwriter. You.'

'Am I right in thinking you listened in to our recording sessions?'

'Through the shower-room wall and outside the door?' He laughed. 'I'd never make a top spy, would I?'

'Nope.'

'One thing,' chipped in Greg. 'If I may? Why did you have such a strong need to know?'

'Well,' said Joey, 'I'd had a pretty lonely childhood. No siblings. And not having the material things my friends had, always made me an outsider.'

'Were you socially ostracised?' asked Greg the psychologist.

'Exactly that. Plus, I also suffered from low-level depression. Genetic, maybe. Who knows. I wished, so often, that I had a brother or sister. They'd be like a ready-made friend, you know?'

'Were you ever suicidal?' Greg ploughed on.

'No, I was never that bad. I'd sometimes joke with Dolores about topping myself if I didn't find out if I had a brother or sister, or if I discovered there wasn't one. "Don't you effing dare," Dol would say, getting all emotional, and I'd say of course I wouldn't. And then it began to happen. I was in the shower room, listening to you and Suzie, and up came Peter, my dad. Honestly, I got goose bumps. And I knew, from her tone, that Suzie would soon admit that *she'd* had the baby, and not her mother. And then I heard her tell you the baby's name.'

'That's enough!' came a deep male voice from the doorway.

I turned. 'Dylan?'

'Christ, he's got a knife,' said Greg.

'Shut up!' Dylan yelled.

'I'm so sorry, Greg,' I whispered. I really had to stop doing this to him. 'I love you, you know.'

'I love you too, but Christ, Edie.'

Dylan came closer. 'I said! Shut! Up!' He put his free hand on my shoulder. 'Give me your phone,' he said, and I took it from my pocket and held it up. 'And you, whoever you are, give me yours.'

'I'm Edie's partner, Greg. Joey has my phone.'

'Dylan, why don't you put that knife down?' called out Joey.

Dylan strode towards him. 'I will when I've heard you telling them your story. Now hand over your phone too.'

Once he'd gathered all three mobiles, Dylan checked they were off, then chucked them, one by one, over the car and into the farthest corner. He then paced up and down in silence, occasionally scratching his head, like someone who'd got halfway through his plan and didn't know where to take it.

'Did you follow Edie?' asked Joey.

Dylan turned to me. 'I put a tracker on your car.'

'When?' I asked, stunned.

'The afternoon you came over, after the party. When I took Suzie up to bed?'

'Ah, right,' I said, recalling him coming back in through the front door. 'But why?'

'Because I thought, at some point, you'd try and find Joey.'

'OK,' I said, 'but why did you want to find him so badly?'

Dylan stopped pacing and look nonplussed. 'Listen, Joey, why don't you carry on telling your story. The one you told me, OK? Including the night of the party.'

Joey wriggled on his passenger seat. 'All right. Mind if I stand and lean against the car?'

'I do mind,' said Dylan with a flicker of the knife. 'Stay where you are.'

'OK, no problem. Right, well, discovering who my half-brother was came as quite a shock.'

'Who?' whispered Greg and I nodded Dylan's way.

'Shit, really?'

Joey sighed heavily. 'All those years of wondering, and researching, and working on Suzie... only to find out my sibling was this arsehole of an entitled dickhead, who'd had everything I hadn't. A private education, Cambridge, a successful business, holidays abroad. The perfect wife and daughter. It was at that point that I seriously thought of ending it all. And what better way to do it than on my birthday, in front of said entitled dickhead.'

Odd, I thought, since he'd just told us he'd never been suicidal. I frowned at Greg. He frowned back.

Dylan was pacing again. 'Tell us about the night of the party, Joey. What you told me.'

Joey shot me a quick look I couldn't read, then sighed again. 'The thing about suicidal people is that they truly believe the world would be better off without them. I wasn't thinking too much about the effect of my jumping on all those people down there at the party. I just wanted to end my life and, hopefully, rock my brother's cosy little world. I'd written a note and left it in my room, covering what I've told you today, and more.'

'But then,' I said, not quite buying his rather monotone story, 'Dolores set off to find you for the cake cutting.'

'Yes. She discovered me bending over the railings of the balcony, about to summersault into the void below. Horrified, she rushed at me from behind and tried to pull me upright. She was a strong woman but couldn't reach my shoulder to tug me back. And so she grabbed a chair to stand on and in her second attempt to grasp me, she fell over me… I heard her cry out but could do nothing. I ran down to my room and locked the door. Luckily, most guests were in the garden to sing *Happy Birthday* and as far as I knew, no one saw me.'

'Joey told me all this the next morning,' said Dylan. 'He was clearly shaken up and determined to leave. With Suzie uppermost in my mind, I insisted it wasn't his fault, and that he should stay at the villa and behave as normally as possible, and that I'd help him find a good therapist.'

When Dylan turned and paced away from us, Joey gave me a definite shake of the head. Dylan was lying. Perhaps he'd kicked Joey out. But why kick him out, then immediately put a tracker on my car to find him? It didn't make sense.

'I pleaded with him to stay,' said Dylan, swivelling around, 'but once the police had come for a daylight search, hoping to find a note from Dolores, Joey loaded up his car and left, saying he'd probably go to a hotel for a couple of nights to think about what to do. Said he'd be in touch but then blocked me on his phone.'

I now put my hand up. 'Could I just ask, Joey, why you buried Dolores's shoe?'

'I'm sorry?' he said, frowning. 'What shoe? Buried where?'

I glanced over at Dylan, who'd stopped in his tracks. Behind him, the bright sunlight coming through the door suddenly got blocked off as yet another person stepped into the barn.

'Dylan!' yelled Emily. 'Drop the knife!'

What the… As my eyes adjusted, I could see she was holding aloft, with both hands, what looked a lot like a gun. This was ridiculous; a dream, surely?

Dylan chuckled. 'Yeah, yeah. I bet it's real and loaded.' He waved the knife in the air, as if to say his weapon was the real deal.

'My husband's a police officer,' Emily said sharply, 'and he's been issued this gun for a murder case. While he was in the shower, I saw where Edie was on my Find My app and had a really bad feeling. So I grabbed the gun and left. My husband's been, like, crazily phoning me.'

'Oh, Emily,' I said. I was impressed with her storytelling and took the baton. 'I know you did that police firearms course and got top marks for target practice, but it might be better for everyone if you put the gun down?'

'Only when Dylan puts the knife down.'

'OK, OK,' said Dylan. 'I'm going to take four steps forward, put the knife down, and take four steps back. All right?'

'OK,' Emily said, 'but make it six.' She kept the gun trained on him until he was back in place. 'You buried the shoe, didn't you, Dylan?'

'I thought you were going to put the gun down?'

'What was on it?' she asked. 'A cigar burn? Or maybe some of that poncy lager you drink? Or just your DNA?'

Dylan snorted. 'I've *no* idea what you're talking about. Anyone could have buried it in the front…' He stopped, realising his error. Had Dylan spotted that the shrub had been moved back to its original place, when he'd pulled into the drive and almost killed Mike and me? Then seen through our ruse – sitting out the front on a non-sunny day?

'And at what point,' continued Emily, 'did you realise you'd left your can of Belgian white beer and a half-smoked cigar up in the attic? Before or after you told the police you hadn't been up there all evening?'

'He was there,' said Joey.

'Shut the fuck up!' shouted Dylan.

'You know what, *bro*?' said Joey. 'I honestly don't give a toss about our agreement. I don't want your money, and I'll gladly own up to selling some of Suzie's things. Do you know how little we were paid? No wait, of course you do. You set up our wages and they never increased. Oh, and just for the record, Dolores seriously disapproved of me taking stuff to sell. We fought about it a lot and I had to force the money on her. Not sure she spent it, mind you.'

Ah, right. The argument I'd heard, those Scrabble letters.

'Stand still, Dylan!' shouted Emily.

'Sorry.' He put his hands in the air.

'I've got video evidence,' she said, 'that immediately after Dolores fell, your fancy beer and a half-smoked cigar were in the attic room on the coffee table.'

'Yeah, he put them down,' said Joey. 'I remember.'

'Two days later, the scene hadn't changed,' said Emily. 'Photos show that everything in the attic or on the balcony had stayed the same. Except for that can of Belgian lager and the cigar, which were no longer there.'

I hadn't yet shared the photos with Emily, only the video. Which meant she must have compared my video and photos on my phone. Today, after ordering the flip chart? While I was glamming myself up for Greg? She must also have set up the Find My tracker between our iPhones.

'All lies!' cried Dylan. 'Listen, are you going to put that police-property gun down?'

'No,' said Emily. 'Do you think I'm mad? Joey, why don't you tell everyone what *actually* happened?'

'OK,' he said, looking directly at me. 'So scrub what I said earlier… all of it.' He took a deep breath. 'Here's what really went on, not what my loving half-brother concocted to save his reputation. Dolores came and found me to say it was time for everyone to sing *Happy Birthday*. I could tell she'd had a bit to drink because she was smiling and chilled. Anyway, I was having a quick spliff on the balcony, and was also feeling pretty relaxed, and what with having had a few beers, I found myself telling her that Dylan was my half-brother, as Suzie had been a teenage mother, and what a huge disappointment it had been discovering that. Dolores was shocked about it, obviously, but then we laughed, and I jokingly said, "Maybe I should end it all now."'

'Maybe you should have,' Dylan said.

'Shut up and let him speak!' yelled Emily. She did angry surprisingly well. 'Carry on, Joey.'

'Right. So it was then that I spotted Dylan behind us in the attic room. I think he'd probably just wandered up from the drawing room to have a smoke and, unfortunately, overheard me. He looked so shocked that I really believed he hadn't known. He said, "How dare you insinuate that about my sister," and then he suddenly became enraged, and he put his drink down and ran at me, and we got into this crazy, comical even, fight on the balcony, which Dolores…' Joey's voice cracked. 'She tried to break it up. Why did she do that?'

'He's lying,' said Dylan, but in a less convincing way, his eyes darting from side to side, like he was trying to plan his escape. 'Absolutely nothing he's saying is true.'

Joey sniffed and shook his head. 'Dylan was stronger than me, and at the point where it felt like I was literally going to go over the edge, Dolores jumped on Dylan and somehow got shrugged off and… and then I heard her cry out as she fell. The reason Dylan tracked you, Edie, was, as he said, that he hoped you'd find me. But it was also so he could keep an eye on me. Make sure I stuck to his fairy-tale story and not implicate him. Isn't that right, bruv?'

Dylan's sudden dash for the knife made me gasp, while beside me Greg jumped to his feet. And as Dylan strode towards Emily, Greg charged at him and Emily screamed, 'No!'

Dylan half-turned just as Greg tackled him to the ground. I heard Greg scream out in pain, and then I heard Emily scream, and then the last scream I heard was mine.

While Joey went to Greg's aid, and Dylan legged it out the door, I stumbled my way around Joey's car on shaking legs, panting and sobbing and hunting for my phone. But at the sound of an approaching siren, and then another, I gave up on the search and hurried towards Greg, face to one side and unmoving on the concrete floor. Emily was kneeling over him, crying.

'We need to stem the flow,' Joey said.

'They'll be here soon, Greg,' sobbed Emily. 'I texted Ben when I was listening outside.'

'Thank God,' I told her. I felt nauseous and willed myself not to throw up the contents of our weird little lunch. I looked anywhere but at Greg's face. I just couldn't.

'Give me the gun?' I asked Emily.

'It's not real,' she sobbed. 'It's Flo's. Suzie gave it to her.'

'I know. Quickly.' I held out my hand and she placed the toy pistol in it. 'You never had the gun, right? Right, Emily? You *never* had a gun!'

'OK.'

'Joey?' I said, holding it up.

'She never had it,' he agreed, taking off his T-shirt to press it against the wound in Greg's side.

As the sirens grew louder, I popped around the side of the barn, opened the boot of my car and buried Flo's gun deep inside a bag of groceries. Then, from a pack of six, I ripped out a small bottle of water, ran back in and handed it to Emily. 'This was what you were holding,' I panted, 'OK?' and she and Joey nodded.

TWENTY-SEVEN

Five weeks later

'Ready?' I asked Greg. He'd insisted on dressing himself, but I'd had to help get his right arm in the shirt sleeve, and then into the suit-jacket sleeve.

He turned back from the mirror and looked me up and down. 'Wow, gorgeous. Love the hat.' It was pinkish red and wide-brimmed, and I'd probably take it off the minute we left the Register Office.

'And you look as handsome as ever,' I said.

Greg did a little bow and went, 'Ouch,' and I grimaced with him, even though I knew he'd been putting it on for weeks. I'd popped back into the flat one time to get my sunglasses and found him doing press-ups. I think he just liked being with me all the time.

'OK, let's go,' I said, 'before I change my mind about this stupid hat.'

* * *

After getting a two-hour parking ticket, we left the wheelchair in the car and Greg used crutches to climb the steps up to the Register Office. In the waiting room were some familiar faces – Emily, Ben and a sleeping Flo amongst them.

'How are you, Greg?' asked Emily.

He would be asked that a lot, I guessed, as this was his first public appearance since the incident. I left him to tell them, and wandered over to Joey.

'Are you liking your new place?' he asked.

'We are, yes.'

While Greg had still been in hospital, I'd found us a ground-floor flat in Summertown. Wheelchair access, private garden and close to the shops – perfect, except for the eye-wateringly high rent. However, we'd probably be all right, financially. Greg had a buyer for the cottage he should no longer climb the winding and hazardous stairs of, and Maeve was selling her Brighton place to her tenants. The plan was she'd buy me out of the house we jointly owned. The one I'd spent my entire adulthood in.

'We love it here, Mum,' she'd said, when presenting the idea to me. 'But I'm not sure you do, not anymore.' She hadn't been wrong.

I'd missed Jesus's visit but was told it went really well. Alfie had been on cloud nine for days, talking about his dad's next visit in September. I prayed daily that Jesus would turn up, and Maeve assured me he would. I could only guess she'd be paying his air fare, and some.

I asked Joey if he and Lily were still together, but apparently she'd moved on to a mate of his on the football team. 'She used to cheer me on,' he said, 'now it's snaky Jake's name she's shouting.' He laughed. 'So much for her being "the one",' he said, making speech marks in the air.

'Would you all like to come through?' asked an official, and we followed her into a wood-panelled room, where Greg and I took end seats because of the crutches he may or may not have still needed. There were about fifty in the audience… or was it a congregation? Party?

I waved at Mike, then Suzie and Peter came through a door to our right, coordinated in shades of pale grey and pink – pink tie on Peter, pink flowers in Suzie's hand, her other one clasping Peter's. I instantly began to cry – weddings! – and didn't stop throughout the ceremony. When they were pronounced husband and wife, we all cheered and Greg leaned my way.

'Should we do this?' he asked.

'Um…' I said, taken aback. I wanted to say yes, but experience had taught me to keep Greg keen. 'I don't think so.'

* * *

At the reception, held in a beautiful room above a pub just outside Oxford, I queued to congratulate the happy couple and tell Suzie how gorgeous she looked. 'You seem so happy, too.'

'I am,' she said dreamily.

'How's that book coming along?'

'Scrapped it!' She gave me big smile. 'I think I was looking for answers that I no longer need.'

Someone behind said, 'Congratulations, Suzie!' and I moved along to Peter.

'What a whirlwind romance!' I said, kissing both his cheeks.

'I'm only going to have whirlwind ones from now on,' he said. 'Such fun.'

'Suzie *is* fun,' I said. 'And funny.'

He laughed. 'We do both tell the most corny jokes.'

'I haven't noticed!'

'Come for dinner soon?'

'We'd love to.'

'Ah, Frank!' he cried, holding out a hand. 'Wonderful that you made it, all the way from the pub.'

I almost expected Dylan to wander in, but of course he wouldn't. Were Peter and Suzie feeling sad about their son's absence? They didn't appear to be anything but loved up.

A few days previously I'd asked how Suzie felt about Dylan not attending the wedding, and she'd claimed to be OK with it. We'd been sitting in her garden while Peter baked.

'To be honest, Edie, I've never really liked him. No, that's too harsh. I resented him, rather. Dylan was a constant reminder of Peter, the blue eyes in particular, and of a horrible time in my life. Because of him, I lost Peter and a school I loved and my good friends. On top of that, he had everything I hadn't. His mother's adoration and attention and, once Daddy had quickly worked his way up the career ladder, a stable and increasingly wealthy home life.'

It had felt very similar to Joey's resentment of his half-brother, and I'd begun to feel sorry for Dylan. He hadn't asked to be born and adored, and in the end he had brought Peter back into Suzie's life.

'Dylan and I spoke on the phone a couple of days ago,' Suzie had added. 'About my having given birth to him. He claimed it had been a dreadful shock, hearing it up in the attic. And I *think* I believe him. You know my mother wanted to tell Dylan the truth, days from the end when she was in hospital. I stopped her that time, but she was wily.' Suzie had smiled at me and shrugged. 'I might never know if she got the message to him.'

'Wow,' I'd said, surprised. Had Dylan known for some time? Had embarrassment, or fearing for his reputation, made him keep the family secret? Going with that theory, had discovering loose-lipped Joey was his half-brother incensed him… made him try to chuck him off the balcony? I'd felt a horrible shiver down my spine. Perhaps we'd given Dylan the benefit of the doubt too readily.

'The great thing is,' Suzie had added, 'Peter instantly liked him. Loved him, even. It seems he's had the parental instincts all these years, while I've had none!'

'I hope Dylan will be all right,' I'd said, meaning *and not kill us all in our beds.*

'Oh, he'll be fine. Business is booming at the restaurants, thanks to the publicity. And maybe he won't get a custodial sentence, in the end.'

'Here's hoping,' I'd agreed, trying not to see Dylan's knife blade, inches from me as I'd handed over my phone.

Joey, Emily and I had played down the events in the barn when giving our statements. We'd all told the police that Emily had misconstrued what had been going on in the barn, when listening outside. And that she'd been carrying a bottle of water, when Dylan had asked her to put what he thought was a gun down. He was short-sighted, and had that visualisation thing… and Emily had had the sun behind her – all of which I'd made sure to slip into my conversation with a police officer. So, our story was that when Greg had gone up to him from behind, Dylan had spun around and accidentally stabbed him, just the once. It was more or less what had happened.

Even Joey had revised his version of the fight on the balcony. 'It was messy,' he'd told me. 'A jumble of bodies and heightened emotions. I can't say for sure what happened. All I remember was Dylan standing there with Dolores's yellow shoe in his hand, looking horrified. Maybe he'd tried to save her by grabbing her foot?'

Understandably, neither he nor Dylan had owned up to the police about having been on that balcony. Dylan – my guess would have been – because his reputation could have been salvageable with only the one charge against him, regarding possession of a knife and threatening behaviour, and Joey because he'd wanted to keep it from Suzie.

'Let me introduce you to my stepson,' Suzie was now saying, an arm around Joey. 'Who's now moved back in.'

'I heard!' I said.

Joey nodded. 'Got my old room again. Oh yeah, Edie, I meant to say I'm going to be a mature student. Follow in Dad's footsteps and do a degree.'

'That's great. In what?'

'Psychology.'

'Ah! Well I know someone who can help you with that.'

'You mean Greg?'

'Yes.'

I looked around, expecting him to be hitting on a waitress, before remembering that was Old Greg. Instead, he was in conversation with Pete DuBarry, who'd decided to go for black leather trousers and a collarless white shirt. It wasn't a bad look.

Lunch was buffet style and after filling our plates, Emily and I sat together and chatted about the agency.

'Do you think you'll be back in action soon?' she asked. 'Or has the thing in the barn put you off?'

'I can't really say when I'll be back.' Emily and Mike had mainly been serving legal papers and following cheating partners in recent weeks. 'And it's not the barn, don't worry. More that Greg needs me at the moment.'

'Yeah, poor guy. I can't help feeling like totally responsible.'

'Don't be daft, Em. We all cocked up. I should never have gone to Rosebud Cottage, let alone taken Greg there. And Joey should never have let himself be bought off by Dylan the morning after the party when he was still in shock. And Dylan, well, he should have just let things be at the villa. Not try and stop Suzie writing her book, for fear of litigation. You know, we could even blame Suzie because she gave Flo a toy gun. We all made mistakes.'

'But not poor Greg, who was only trying to save me.'

'True.'

'You know, I'm not even sure Dylan was coming for me. Maybe he was aiming for the door behind me.'

I shrugged, now unsure about pretty much everything. 'Whatever you do, don't tell Greg that.'

'I wouldn't, don't worry. I reckon he should get a medal, though.'

'You mean for living with me? I can be a bit bossy!'

'Can't say I've noticed, ha ha.' She waved across the room at Flo, up on Ben's shoulders. 'Oh, yeah, I got an unusual enquiry from a woman who thinks her husband's cheating on her.'

'That's unusual?'

'There's more. She's, like, a friend of Astrid's.'

I hadn't heard from Astrid since before her failed interview. She was unembarrassable, so it couldn't have been that. She'd be in touch if she needed me, or vice versa.

'So,' Emily was saying, 'I called her just to check this woman wasn't a scammer, and Astrid said she knew her well from working in London together and that she, this woman, was making a fortune on some Only Fans type thing.'

'Oh!' I said, my first thought being why hard-up Astrid didn't do that. Or perhaps she was. Maybe it was taking up all her time and I'd fallen off her radar? 'And is she in Oxford? This friend?'

'Uh-uh. The Canary Islands. She's actually offering all expenses paid in a luxury hotel, and a free translator.'

'Blimey!' What on earth had Astrid said about me, and could I possibly live up to it now my confidence had taken a hit? Mind you, Greg deserved a break. And he spoke excellent Spanish. He loved Real Madrid and Rioja. And hadn't we talked about going to see the sea, just the other day? Why not switch Worthing for Las Palmas?

'Could you forward me the email?' I asked Emily.

'Just did,' she said, with a smirk. 'Gonna add mind reading to my psychic skills.'

* * *

An hour or so later, I had Joey sitting on one side of me, and Greg on the other. There were no formal speeches, but Peter stood up, tapped a glass with a fork, and asked if he could say a few words. He began by thanking everyone for coming along, and praised those who'd organised the reception.

'Why not?' Greg asked me, as Peter continued.

'I just don't see myself marrying,' I whispered. A woman told us to shush. 'But thanks for proposing,' I quickly added.

'You're welcome.'

We listened to Peter eulogising about Suzie and touching briefly on their teenage love and recent rediscovery of one another.

I leaned towards Greg. 'I know of an all-expenses-paid pretend honeymoon we could go on, though.'

'Where?'

'Canaries. Fancy it?'

'Er, yeah. Let's do it.' Greg was too trusting for his own good. 'I might get to jump queues at the airport.'

When Peter had run out of superlatives for Suzie, he raised his glass. 'I've got the best wife in England,' he said, kissing her cheek then winking at his audience. 'The other one's in Spain.'

'Tommy Cooper,' whispered Joey, before the laughter broke out.

If you enjoyed this book, please let others know by leaving a quick review on Amazon. Also, if you spot anything untoward in the paperback, get in touch. We strive for the best quality and appreciate reader feedback.

editor@thebookfolks.com

www.thebookfolks.com

Also in this series

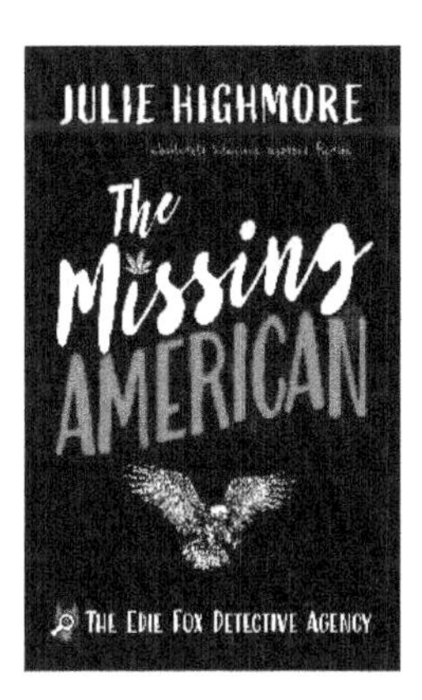

THE MISSING AMERICAN (Book 1)

Edie Fox is more than a little suspicious when a wealthy American turns up to her cluttered backstreet office in Oxford, England, and hands her a bundle of cash to find his missing cousin. But not enough to turn down the deal. Yet she soon has more on her hands than she bargained for when an old flame enters her life, and the witnesses in her case start giving her the run-around.

FREE with Kindle Unlimited and available in paperback!

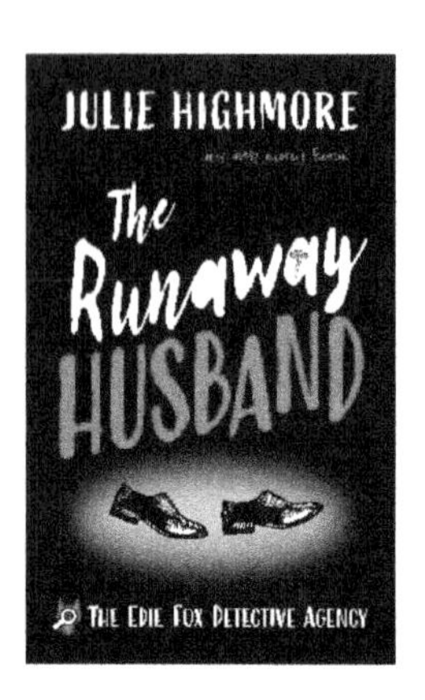

THE RUNAWAY HUSBAND (Book 2)

Edie Fox is secretly resentful of her glamorous new client, Jessica Relish, who comes into her Oxford detective agency searching for her missing husband. But when the much younger, and apparently handsome and charming Hugh turns up dead in a wood, Edie's jealousy vanishes, and she quickens the search to find out what happened to him.

FREE with Kindle Unlimited and available in paperback!

Other titles of interest

MURDER ON A COUNTRY LANE
by Jon Harris

After the shock of discovering a murder victim, young barmaid Julia isn't too perturbed because local garden centre owner Audrey White was a horrible so-and-so. But when her fingerprints are found all over a death threat, Julia becomes the police's prime suspect. Equipped with an unfetching ankle tag she must solve the crime to prove her innocence.

FREE with Kindle Unlimited and available in paperback!

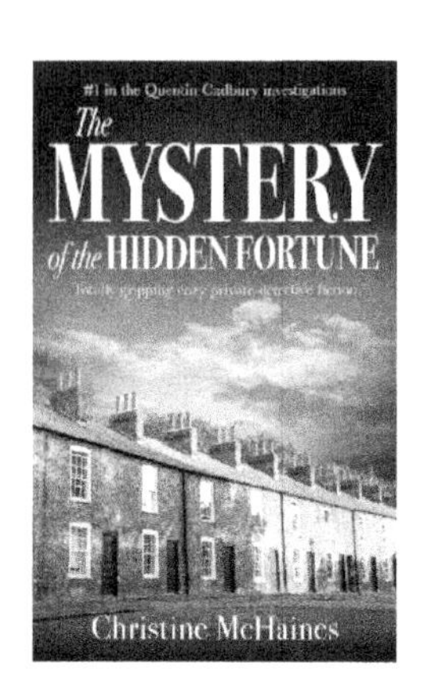

THE MYSTERY OF THE HIDDEN FORTUNE
by Christine McHaines

Quentin Cadbury, a useless twenty-something, is left to look after his late aunt's London house when his parents head to Australia. But burglars seem determined to break in, and not even the stray cat he befriends can help him. As the thieves are after something pretty valuable, and illegal, he must grow up pretty fast to get out of a sticky situation.

FREE with Kindle Unlimited and available in paperback!

THE
BOOK
FOLKS

Printed in Great Britain
by Amazon